PUFFIN

DAVID COPPERFIELD

'If you please, aunt, I am your nephew.'

'Oh, Lord!' said my aunt. And sat flat down in the garden-path.

'I am David Copperfield, of Blunderstone, in Suffolk – where you came, on the night when I was born, and saw my dear mama. I have been very unhappy since she died. I have been slighted, and taught nothing, and thrown upon myself, and put to work not fit for me. It made me run away to you. I have walked all the way, and have never slept in a bed since I began the journey.'

CHARLES DICKENS

DAVID COPPERFIELD

Abridged by **NEVILLE TELLER**

INTRODUCED BY
CHRISTOPHER PAOLINI

PUFFIN

PUFFIN BOOKS

Published by the Penguin Group
Penguin Books Ltd, 80 Strand, London WC2R ORL, England
Penguin Group (USA) Inc., 375 Hudson Street, New York, New York 10014, USA
Penguin Group (Canada), 90 Eglinton Avenue East, Suite 700, Toronto, Ontario, Canada M4P 2Y3
(a division of Pearson Penguin Canada Inc.)
Penguin Ireland, 25 St Stephen's Green, Dublin 2, Ireland (a division of Penguin Books Ltd)
Penguin Group (Australia), 707 Collins Street, Melbourne, Victoria 3008, Australia
(a division of Pearson Australia Group Pty Ltd)
Penguin Books India Pvt Ltd, 11 Community Centre, Panchsheel Park, New Delhi – 110 017, India
Penguin Group (NZ), 67 Apollo Drive, Rosedale, Auckland 0632, New Zealand
(a division of Pearson New Zealand Ltd)
Penguin Books (South Africa) (Pty) Ltd, Block D, Rosebank Office Park, 181 Jan Smuts Avenue,
Parktown North, Gauteng 2193, South Africa

Penguin Books Ltd, Registered Offices: 80 Strand, London WC2R ORL, England

puffinbooks.com

First published 1850
This abridgement first published in Penguin Books 2001
Published in this edition 2012
004

Abridgement text copyright © Penguin Books, 2001, 2012
Introduction copyright © Christopher Paolini, 2012
Endpages copyright © Penguin Books, 2012
All rights reserved

The moral right of Christopher Paolini has been asserted

Set in 11.5/15 pt Minion Pro
Typeset by Palimpsest Book Production Limited, Falkirk, Stirlingshire
Printed in Great Britain by Clays Ltd, St Ives plc

British Library Cataloguing in Publication Data
A CIP catalogue record for this book is available from the British Library

ISBN: 978-0-141-34382-2

www.greenpenguin.co.uk

MIX
Paper from
responsible sources
FSC
www.fsc.org   FSC™ C018179

Penguin Books is committed to a sustainable
future for our business, our readers and our planet.
This book is made from Forest Stewardship
Council™ certified paper.

CHRISTOPHER PAOLINI

This book scared the pants off me.

For whatever reason, my mother chose to read *David Copperfield* to my sister and me when I was around ten or eleven. After the relative airy lightness of Jane Austen, the world of Dickens seemed dark and monstrous. Even to this day, I remain convinced that it would be hard to write a more frightening book for a child without delving even further into outright physical abuse. The thought of being unable to count on the adults in your life – on your very parents, or step-parents – of being thrashed for failing to keep up with your studies, of being sent away to a strange and unfriendly boarding school, and then of being put to work in a factory far from home . . . what could be more terrifying when you are young and still at the mercy of those who are supposed to be your carers?

More than a decade and a half later, the prospect still sends a chill through me, right through to the bone.

The trials and tribulations to which Dickens subjected the young David Copperfield, of course, reflected a great deal of his own life. At the age of twelve, when one ought to be able to count on the stability of family, Dickens's world was torn apart, with his father sent to debtors' prison and Dickens himself forced to leave school and work in Warren's Blacking warehouse. From this, it seems obvious, springs the profound sense of abandonment, hostility, alienation and sadness that permeates the first part of this book, all the way until David Copperfield finds sanctuary with his only remaining relative, his great-aunt Miss Betsey Trotwood.

And yet, even then, a sense of unease about the solidity of the world remains. Mr Micawber constantly struggles with financial difficulty. Steerforth proves to be a cad of the worst sort. And Uriah Heep, that most 'umble of men, plots against his employer, Mr Wickfield. Along with the weakness and villainy of those around him, David Copperfield must also contend with the cruel blows of impersonal fate, which strike down his first wife, Dora.

So, *David Copperfield* is a superbly written horror novel. But it is also enormously funny and filled with Dickens's trademark wit and facility. Moreover, it contains the single best piece of financial advice in history, delivered courtesy of Mr Micawber, who observes 'that if a man had twenty pounds a-year for his income, and spent nineteen pounds nineteen shillings and sixpence, he would be happy, but that if he spent twenty pounds one he would be miserable'.

This again reflects Dickens's own life, as it is a close paraphrase of something his father told him.

David Copperfield is one of Dickens's two greatest novels, the other being *Great Expectations*. Which you prefer is a matter of personal taste, but both contain a multitude of riches. *David Copperfield* is a classic coming-of-age story, and in it we watch as Copperfield himself learns to strike a balance between the unyielding sternness of Mr Murdstone and the impulsive (though kind) ways of Mr Micawber. Like all the best fiction, *David Copperfield* deals with universal human experiences and Dickens does it so artfully that few can help but empathize with the experiences of the main character.

I never did finish the book as a child. I was too frightened. However, I returned to it as an adult and read it with new-found pleasure and appreciation. The characters are indelible, the prose masterful and the story itself incredibly affecting. The clink of Miss Murdstone's steel beads, the clamminess of Uriah Heep's palm, Mrs Gummidge's plaintive cry of 'lone lorn creetur' . . . all these things (and more) have become as much a part of my life and memory as any real event. I cannot recommend the book enough. It is one of the truest representations of what it means to be human.

Just don't read it to a very young kid. It'll scare the pants off them. I guarantee it.

1

To begin my life with the beginning of my life, I record that I was born (as I have been informed and believe) on a Friday, at twelve o'clock at night at Blunderstone, in Suffolk. I was a posthumous child. My father's eyes had closed upon the light of this world six months, when mine opened on it.

An aunt of my father's, and consequently a great-aunt of mine, was the principal magnate of our family – Miss Trotwood, or Miss Betsey, as my poor mother always called her, when she sufficiently overcame her dread of this formidable personage to mention her at all.

My father had once been a favourite of hers, I believe; but she was mortally affronted by his marriage, on the ground that my mother, whom she had never seen, was not yet twenty. My father and Miss Betsey never met again.

This was the state of matters on the afternoon of, what I may be excused for calling, that eventful and important Friday.

My mother was sitting by the fire, but poorly in health

and very low in spirits, looking at it through her tears, when, lifting her eyes as she dried them to the window opposite, she saw a strange lady coming up the garden.

My mother had a sure foreboding at the second glance, that it was Miss Betsey. She went and opened the door.

'Mrs David Copperfield, I think,' said Miss Betsey.

'Yes.'

'Miss Trotwood,' said the visitor. 'You have heard of her, I dare say?'

My mother answered she had had that pleasure.

'Now you see her,' said Miss Betsey. My mother begged her to walk in.

They went into the parlour my mother had come from, the fire in the best room on the other side of the passage not being lighted. When they were both seated, Miss Betsey said:

'Well, and when do you expect . . .?'

'I am all in a tremble,' faltered my mother. 'I don't know what's the matter.'

'Have some tea,' said Miss Betsey.

'Oh dear me, do you think it will do me any good?' cried my mother.

'Of course it will,' said Miss Betsey. 'It's nothing but fancy. What do you call your girl?'

'I don't know that it will be a girl, yet, ma'am,' said my mother innocently.

'Bless the Baby!' exclaimed Miss Betsey, unconsciously

quoting the second sentiment of the pincushion in the drawer upstairs. 'I don't mean that. I mean your servant-girl.'

'Peggotty,' said my mother.

'Here! Peggotty!' cried Miss Betsey, opening the parlour door. 'Tea. Your mistress is a little unwell. Don't dawdle.'

Having issued this mandate, Miss Betsey shut the door again, and sat down as before, with her feet on the fender.

'You were speaking about its being a girl,' said Miss Betsey. 'I have no doubt it will be a girl. Now, child, from the moment of the birth of this girl . . .'

'Perhaps boy,' my mother took the liberty of putting in.

'I tell you I have a presentiment that it must be a girl,' returned Miss Betsey. 'From the moment of this girl's birth, child, I intend to be her friend. I intend to be her godmother, and I beg you'll call her Betsey Trotwood Copperfield.'

When, later that same day, my mother was delivered of a boy, my aunt walked out, and never came back. She vanished like a discontented fairy. I lay in my basket, and my mother lay in her bed; but Betsey Trotwood Copperfield was for ever in the land of dreams and shadows.

2

The first objects that assume a distinct presence before me, as I look far back into the blank of my infancy, are my mother with her pretty hair and youthful shape, and Peggotty with no shape at all.

What else do I remember? Let me see. There comes out of the cloud, our house. On the ground-floor is Peggotty's kitchen, opening into a back yard. Here is a long passage – what an enormous perspective I make of it! – leading from Peggotty's kitchen to the front door.

Here is our pew in the church. With a window near it, out of which our house can be seen, and is seen many times during the morning's service.

And now I see the outside of our house, with the latticed bedroom-windows standing open to let in the sweet-smelling air.

Peggotty and I were sitting one night by the parlour fire, alone, when the garden-bell rang. We went out to the door, and there was my mother, looking unusually pretty, I thought, and with her a gentleman with beautiful black hair and whiskers, who had walked home with us from church last Sunday.

As my mother stooped down on the threshold to take me in her arms and kiss me, the gentleman said I was a more highly privileged little fellow than a monarch – or something like that – and patted me on the head, but somehow I didn't like him, or his deep voice, and I put his hand away.

Whether it was the following Sunday when I saw the gentleman again, or whether there was any greater lapse of time before he re-appeared, I cannot recall. But there he was, in church, and he walked home with us afterwards.

Gradually, I became used to seeing the gentleman with the black whiskers. I liked him no better than at first – Mr Murdstone – I knew him by that name now.

We were sitting one evening (when my mother was out), when Peggotty, after looking at me several times, said:

'Master Davy, how should you like to go along with me and spend a fortnight at my brother's at Yarmouth? There's the sea; and the boats; and the fishermen; and the beach; and Am to play with –'

Peggotty meant her nephew Ham.

I was flushed by her summary of delights, and replied that it would indeed be a treat, but what would my mother say?

'Why then, I'll as good as bet a guinea,' said Peggotty, 'that she'll let us go. I'll ask her, if you like, as soon as ever she comes home.'

Without being nearly so much surprised as I had expected, my mother entered into it readily.

The day soon came for our going. We were to go in a carrier's cart, which departed in the morning after breakfast.

3

When we saw Yarmouth and the whole adjacent prospect lying a straight low line under the sky, I hinted to Peggotty that a mound or so might have improved it. But Peggotty said, with greater emphasis than usual, that we must take things as we found them, and that for her part Yarmouth was, upon the whole, the finest place in the universe.

'And here's my Am!' she screamed, 'growed out of knowledge!'

He was waiting for us, in fact, at the public-house; and asked me how I found myself, like an old acquaintance. Our intimacy was much advanced by his taking me on his back to carry me home. We went past gas-works, rope-walks, boat-builders' yards, smiths' forges, and a great litter of such places, until Ham said:

'Yon's our house, Mas'r Davy!'

I looked in all directions, but no house could I make out. There was a black barge, not far off, high and dry on the ground, with an iron funnel sticking out of it for a chimney and smoking very cosily.

'That's not it?' said I. 'That ship-looking thing?'

'That's it, Mas'r Davy,' returned Ham.

If it had been Aladdin's palace, I suppose I could not have been more charmed with the romantic idea of living in it.

It was beautifully clean inside, and as tidy as possible. There was a table, and a Dutch clock, and a chest of drawers, and on the chest of drawers there was a tea-tray with a painting on it of a lady with a parasol. Some lockers and boxes served for seats and eked out the chairs.

All this I saw in the first glance after I crossed the threshold, and then Peggotty opened a little door and showed me my bedroom. It was the completest and most desirable bedroom ever seen – in the stern of the vessel, with a little window, where the rudder used to go through. The walls were whitewashed as white as milk, and the patchwork counterpane made my eyes quite ache with its brightness.

We were welcomed by a very civil woman in a white apron, and a most beautiful little girl (or I thought her so) called little Em'ly. By and by, when we had dined in a sumptuous manner off boiled dabs, melted butter, and potatoes, with a chop for me, a hairy man with a very good-natured face came home. As he called Peggotty 'Lass', and gave her a hearty smack on the cheek, I had no doubt that he was her brother.

'Glad to see you, sir,' said Mr Peggotty. 'You'll find us rough, sir, but you'll find us ready.'

I thanked him, and replied that I was sure I should be happy in such a delightful place.

After tea, when the door was shut and all was made snug, it seemed to me the most delicious retreat that the imagination of man could conceive. To hear the wind getting up out at sea, to know that the fog was creeping over the desolate flat outside, and to look at the fire, and think that there was no house near but this one, and this one a boat, was like enchantment. Little Em'ly was sitting by my side; the lady with the white apron was knitting on the opposite side of the fire. Peggotty was at her needle-work; Ham was trying to recollect a scheme of telling fortunes with cards; Mr Peggotty was smoking his pipe.

Later that night, in the privacy of my own little cabin, Peggotty informed me that Ham and Em'ly were an orphan nephew and niece, whom my host had at different times adopted in their childhood, when they were left destitute; and that the lady in the white apron was Mrs Gummidge, the widow of his partner in a boat, who had died very poor.

Of course, I was in love with little Em'ly.

We used to walk about Yarmouth in a loving manner, hours and hours. The days sported by us. I told Em'ly I adored her, and that unless she confessed she adored me, I should be reduced to the necessity of killing myself with a sword. She said she did, and I have no doubt she did. We were the admiration of Mrs Gummidge and Peggotty, who used to whisper of an evening when we sat, lovingly, on our little locker, side by side.

I soon found out that Mrs Gummidge did not always

make herself so agreeable as she might have been expected to do, under the circumstances of her residence with Mr Peggotty.

Mr Peggotty went occasionally to a public-house called The Willing Mind. I discovered this, by his being out on the second or third evening of our visit.

Mrs Gummidge had been in a low state all day, and had burst into tears in the forenoon, when the fire smoked.

'I am a lone lorn creetur',' were Mrs Gummidge's words, 'and everythink goes contrairy with me.'

'Oh, it'll soon leave off,' said Peggotty, 'and besides, you know, it's not more disagreeable to you than to us.'

'I feel it more,' said Mrs Gummidge.

Mrs Gummidge's peculiar corner of the fireside seemed to me to be the warmest and snuggest in the place, but she was constantly complaining of the cold. At last she shed tears on that subject, and said again that she was 'a lone lorn creetur' and everythink went contrairy with her'.

'It is certainly very cold,' said Peggotty. 'Everybody must feel it so.'

'I feel it more than other people,' said Mrs Gummidge.

Accordingly, when Mr Peggotty came home about nine o'clock, this unfortunate Mrs Gummidge was knitting in her corner, in a very wretched and miserable condition.

'What's amiss?' said Mr Peggotty, with a clap of his hands.

Mrs Gummidge took out an old black silk handkerchief and wiped her eyes.

'You've come from The Willing Mind, Dan'l?'

'Why yes, I've took a short spell at The Willing Mind tonight.'

'I'm sorry I should drive you there,' said Mrs Gummidge.

'Drive! I don't want no driving,' returned Mr Peggotty. 'I only go too ready.'

'Very ready,' said Mrs Gummidge, shaking her head, and wiping her eyes. 'I am sorry it should be along of me that you're so ready.'

'Along o'you! It an't along o'you!'

'Yes, yes, it is,' cried Mrs Gummidge. 'I know what I am. I know that I am a lone lorn creetur', and not only that everythink goes contrary with me, but that I go contrary with everybody. Yes, yes. I feel more than other people do, and I show it more. It's my misfortun'.'

Mrs Gummidge retired with these words, and betook herself to bed.

When she was gone, Mr Peggotty looked round upon us, and said:

'She's been thinking of the old 'un!'

And whenever Mrs Gummidge was overcome in a similar manner during the remainder of our stay (which happened some few times), he always said the same thing in extenuation of the circumstance, and always with the tenderest commiseration.

So the fortnight slipped away, and at last the day came for going home. I bore up against the separation from Mr

Peggotty and Mrs Gummidge, but my agony of mind at leaving little Em'ly was piercing.

Now, all the time I had been on my visit, I had thought little or nothing about my home, but the nearer we drew, the more excited I was to get there, and to run into my mother's arms.

The door opened, and I looked, half laughing and half crying in my pleasant agitation, for my mother. It was not she, but a strange servant.

'Why, Peggotty!' I said, ruefully, 'isn't she come home?'

'Yes, yes, Master Davy,' said Peggotty. 'She's come home.'

She took me by the hand; led me, wondering, into the kitchen; and shut the door.

'Peggotty!' said I, quite frightened. 'What's the matter?'

'Nothing's the matter, bless you, Master Davy dear!' she answered, untying her bonnet with a shaking hand. 'What do you think? You've got a pa! A new one.'

'A new one?' I repeated.

Peggotty put out her hand. 'Come and see him.'

'I don't want to see him.'

– 'And your mama,' said Peggotty.

I ceased to draw back, and we went straight to the best parlour, where she left me.

On one side of the fire, sat my mother; on the other, Mr Murdstone. My mother dropped her work, and arose hurriedly, but timidly, I thought.

'Now, Clara, my dear,' said Mr Murdstone. 'Recollect! control yourself. Davy boy, how do you do?'

I gave him my hand. After a moment of suspense, I went and kissed my mother: she kissed me, patted me gently on the shoulder, and sat down again to her work. I could not look at her, I could not look at him, I turned to the window and looked out there, at some shrubs that were drooping their heads in the cold.

As soon as I could creep away, I crept upstairs.

4

Next evening we dined alone, we three together. He seemed to be very fond of my mother – I am afraid I liked him none the better for that – and she was very fond of him. I gathered from what they said, that an elder sister of his was coming to stay with them, and that she was expected that evening.

After dinner, when we were sitting by the fire, a coach drove up to the garden-gate, and he went out to receive the visitor.

It was Miss Murdstone who was arrived, and a gloomy-looking lady she was; dark, like her brother, and with very heavy eyebrows, nearly meeting over her large nose.

She was brought into the parlour with many tokens of welcome, and there formally recognized my mother as a new and near relation. Then she looked at me, and said:

'Is that your boy, sister-in-law?'

My mother acknowledged me.

'Generally speaking,' said Miss Murdstone, 'I don't like boys.'

As well as I could make out, she had come for good, and had no intention of ever going again.

On the very first morning after her arrival she was up at cock-crow. When my mother came down to breakfast and was going to make the tea, Miss Murdstone gave her a kind of peck on the cheek, which was her nearest approach to a kiss, and said:

'Now, Clara, my dear, I am come here, you know, to relieve you of all the trouble I can. You're much too pretty and thoughtless' – my mother blushed but laughed – 'to have any duties imposed upon you that can be undertaken by me. If you'll be so good as give me your keys, my dear, I'll attend to all this sort of thing in the future.'

From that time, Miss Murdstone kept the keys.

My mother did not suffer her authority to pass from her without a shadow of protest. One night, when Miss Murdstone had been developing certain household plans to her brother, of which he signified his approbation, my mother suddenly began to cry.

'It's very hard,' she said, 'that in my own house . . .'

'My own house?' repeated Mr Murdstone. 'Clara!'

'Our own house, I mean,' faltered my mother, evidently frightened. 'It's very hard that in your own house, I may not have a word to say about domestic matters. I am sure I managed very well before we were married.'

'Edward,' said Miss Murdstone, 'let there be an end of this. I go to-morrow.'

'Jane Murdstone,' thundered Mr Murdstone. 'Will you be silent? How dare you? Clara,' he continued, looking at my mother, 'you astound me! Yes, I had a satisfaction in the thought of marrying an artless person, and forming her character. But when Jane Murdstone is kind enough to come to my assistance in this endeavour, and to assume, for my sake, a condition something like a housekeeper's, and when she meets with a base return . . .'

'Oh, pray, pray, Edward,' cried my mother, 'don't accuse me of being ungrateful. I am sure I am not ungrateful. I have a great many defects, I know, and it's very good of you, Edward, with your strength of mind, to endeavour to correct them for me. Jane, I don't object to anything. I should be quite broken-hearted if you thought of leaving . . .'

My mother was too much overcome to go on.

There had been some talk on occasions of my going to boarding-school. Nothing, however, was concluded on the subject yet. In the meantime, I learnt lessons at home.

Shall I ever forget those lessons! They were presided over nominally by my mother, but really by Mr Murdstone and his sister, who were always present. I had been apt enough to learn, and willing enough, when my mother and I had lived alone together. But these solemn lessons which succeeded those, I remember as the death-blow of my peace, and a grievous daily drudgery of misery.

As to any recreation with other children of my age, I had very little of that; for the gloomy theology of the Murdstones made all children out to be a swarm of little vipers and held that they contaminated one another.

The natural result of this treatment – continued, I suppose, for some six months or more – was to make me sullen and dull. I was not made the less so by my sense of being daily more and more shut out and alienated from my mother. I believe I should have been almost stupefied but for one circumstance.

My father had left a small collection of books in a little room upstairs, to which I had access (for it adjoined my own) and which nobody else in our house ever troubled. From that blessed little room came out a glorious host, to keep me company. They kept alive my fancy, and my hope of something beyond that place and time.

One morning, when I went into the parlour with my books, I found my mother looking anxious, Miss Murdstone looking firm, and Mr Murdstone binding something round the bottom of a cane – a lithe and limber cane, which he left off binding when I came in, and poised and switched in the air.

'I tell you, Clara,' said Mr Murdstone, 'I have often been flogged myself.'

'To be sure; of course,' said Miss Murdstone.

I felt apprehensive and sought Mr Murdstone's eye as it lighted on mine.

'Now, David,' he said, 'you must be far more careful today than usual.'

He gave the cane another switch; and laid it down beside him. I felt the words of my lessons slipping off. We began badly, and went on worse. Book after book was added to the heap of failures. At last he rose and took up the cane.

'We can hardly expect Clara to bear, with perfect firmness, the worry and torment that David has occasioned her today. David, you and I will go upstairs, boy.'

As he took me out at the door, my mother ran towards us. Miss Murdstone said:

'Clara! are you a perfect fool?'

I saw my mother stop her ears then, and I heard her crying.

He walked me up to my room slowly and gravely – I am certain he had a delight in the formal parade of executing justice – and when we got there, suddenly twisted my head under his arm.

'Mr Murdstone! Sir!' I cried to him. 'Don't! Pray don't beat me! I have tried to learn, sir, but I can't while you and Miss Murdstone are by. I can't indeed!'

'Can't you, indeed, David?' he said. 'We'll try that.'

And he cut me heavily. In the same instant I caught the hand with which he held me in my mouth, between my teeth, and bit it through.

He beat me then, as if he would have beaten me to death. Above all the noise we made, I heard them running up the stairs, and crying out – I heard my mother crying out – and Peggotty. Then he was gone; and the door was locked outside; and I was lying, fevered and hot, and torn, and sore, and raging in my puny way, upon the floor.

My imprisonment lasted five days. The length of those five days occupy the place of years in my remembrance.

On the last night of my restraint, I was awakened by hearing my own name spoken in a whisper. I groped my way to the door and put my lips to the keyhole.

'Is that you, Peggotty dear?'

'Yes, my own precious Davy. Be as soft as a mouse.'

'What is going to be done with me, Peggotty dear? Do you know?'

'School. Near London,' was Peggotty's answer.

In the morning Miss Murdstone appeared and told me that when I was dressed, I was to come downstairs into the parlour, and have my breakfast. There I found my mother, very pale and with red eyes, into whose arms I ran.

'Oh, Davy!' she said. 'That you could hurt anyone I love! I am so grieved, that you should have such bad passions in your heart.'

They had persuaded her that I was a wicked fellow, and she was more sorry for that than for my going away.

I tried to eat my parting breakfast, but my tears dropped upon my bread-and-butter, and trickled into my tea.

'Master Copperfield's box there!' said Miss Murdstone, when wheels were heard at the gate.

I looked for Peggotty, but neither she nor Mr Murdstone appeared.

'Clara!' said Miss Murdstone, in her warning note.

'Ready, my dear Jane,' returned my mother. 'I forgive you, my dear boy. God bless you!'

'Clara!' repeated Miss Murdstone.

Then I got into the cart, and the lazy horse walked off with it.

5

W e might have gone about half a mile, and my pocket-handkerchief was quite wet through, when the carrier stopped short.

Looking out to ascertain for what, I saw, to my amazement, Peggotty burst from a hedge and climb into the cart. She took me in both her arms, and squeezed me to her stays. She brought out some paper bags of cakes which she crammed into my pockets, and a purse which she put into my hand, but not one word did she say. After another and a final squeeze with both arms, she got down from the cart and ran away.

I had now leisure to examine the purse. It had three bright shillings in it, which Peggotty had evidently polished up with whitening, for my greater delight. But its most precious contents were two half-crowns folded together in a bit of paper, on which was written, in my mother's hand, 'For Davy. With my love.'

After we had jogged on for some little time, I asked the carrier if he was going all the way.

'Why, that horse,' said the carrier, 'would be deader than pork afore he got over half the ground.'

'Are you only going to Yarmouth, then?'

'That's about it,' said the carrier. 'And there I shall take you to the stage-cutch, and the stage-cutch that'll take you to – wherever it is.'

As this was a great deal for the carrier (whose name was Mr Barkis) to say, I offered him a cake as a mark of attention, which he ate at one gulp, exactly like an elephant.

'Did *she* make 'em, now?' said Mr Barkis, always leaning forward, in his slouching way, on the footboard of the cart with an arm on each knee.

'Peggotty, do you mean, sir?'

'Ah!' said Mr Barkis. 'Her.'

'Yes. She makes all our pastry, and does all our cooking.'

'Do she though?' said Mr Barkis.

He sat looking at the horse's ears for a considerable time. By and by, he said:

'No sweethearts, I b'lieve?'

'Oh, no. She never had a sweetheart.'

'Didn't she, though!' said Mr Barkis.

Again he sat looking at the horse's ears.

I replied that such was the fact.

'Well. I'll tell you what,' said Mr Barkis. 'P'raps you might be writin' to her?'

'Oh, I shall certainly write to her.'

'Ah!' he said, slowly turning his eyes towards me. 'Well!

If you was writin' her, p'raps you'd recollect to say that Barkis was willin'; would you?'

'That Barkis is willing,' I repeated, innocently. 'Is that all the message?'

'Ye-es,' he said, 'Barkis is willin'.'

I readily undertook its transmission. While I was waiting for the coach in the hotel at Yarmouth that very afternoon, I procured a sheet of paper and an inkstand, and wrote a note to Peggotty, which ran thus: 'My dear Peggotty. I have come here safe. Barkis is willing. My love to mama. Yours affectionately. P.S. He says he particularly wants you to know – Barkis is willing.'

We started from Yarmouth at three o'clock in the afternoon, and we were due in London about eight next morning.

The night was not pleasant, for it got chilly; and being put between two gentlemen to prevent my tumbling off the coach, I was nearly smothered by their falling asleep, and completely blocking me up.

What an amazing place London was to me when I saw it in the distance. We approached it by degrees, and got, in due time, to the inn in the Whitechapel district, for which we were bound.

A ladder was brought, and I got down after a lady who was like a haystack. The coach was clear of passengers by that time; the luggage was very soon cleared out, the horses had been taken out before the luggage, and now the coach itself was wheeled and backed off by some hostlers, out of the way. Still nobody appeared to claim the dusty youngster from Blunderstone, Suffolk.

More solitary than Robinson Crusoe, I went into the booking-office and, by invitation of the clerk on duty, passed behind the counter and sat down on the scale at which they weighed the luggage. After a while a man entered and whispered to the clerk, who presently slanted me off the scale, and pushed me over to him, as if I were weighed, bought, delivered, and paid for.

As I went out of the office, hand in hand with this new acquaintance, I stole a look at him. He was a gaunt, sallow young man, with hollow cheeks.

'You're the new boy?' he said.

'Yes, sir,' I said.

I supposed I was. I didn't know.

'I'm one of the masters at Salem House,' he said, and told the clerk that the carrier had instructions to call for my box at noon.

A short walk brought us to Salem House, which was enclosed with a high brick wall, and looked very dull. The door was opened by a stout man with a bull-neck, a wooden leg, overhanging temples, and his hair cut close all around his head.

'The new boy,' said the master, whose name was Mr Mell.

All about was so very quiet, that I said to Mr Mell I supposed the boys were out; but he seemed surprised at my not knowing that it was holiday-time, and that Mr Creakle, the proprietor, was down by the sea-side with Mrs and Miss Creakle.

I gazed upon the schoolroom into which he took me, as the most forlorn and desolate place I had ever seen. A long room with three long rows of desks and six of forms, and bristling all round with pegs for hats and slates.

Mr Mell having left me while he went upstairs, I went softly to the upper end of the room. Suddenly I came upon a pasteboard placard, beautifully written, which was lying on the desk, and bore these words: '*Take care of him. He bites.*'

I got upon the desk immediately, apprehensive of at least a great dog underneath. I was still engaged in peering about, when Mr Mell came back, and asked me what I did up there?

'I beg your pardon, sir,' says I, 'if you please, I'm looking for the dog that bites.'

'No, Copperfield,' says he, 'that's not a dog. That's a boy. My instructions are, Copperfield, to put this placard on your back. I am sorry to make such a beginning with you, but I must do it.'

With that he took me down, and tied the placard on my shoulders like a knapsack.

What I suffered from that placard, nobody can imagine. Whether it was possible for people to see me or not, I always fancied that somebody was reading it. That cruel man with the wooden leg aggravated my sufferings. He was in authority; and if ever he saw me leaning against a tree, or a wall, or the house, he roared out from his lodge door:

'Hallo, you sir! You Copperfield! Show that badge conspicuous, or I'll report you!'

I knew that the servants read it, and the butcher read it, and the baker read it; I recollect that I positively began to have a dread of myself, as a kind of wild boy who did bite.

6

One day I was informed by Mr Mell that Mr Creakle would be home that evening. Before bedtime, I was fetched by the man with the wooden leg to appear before him.

'So!' said Mr Creakle. 'This is the young gentleman whose teeth are to be filed! Turn him round.'

The wooden-legged man turned me about so as to exhibit the placard; and having afforded time for a full survey of it, turned me about again, with my face to Mr Creakle. Mr Creakle's face was fiery, and his eyes were small and deep in his head; he had a little nose, and a large chin.

'Come here, sir!' said Mr Creakle, beckoning to me. 'I have the happiness of knowing your father-in-law,' taking me by the ear. 'He is a man of a strong character.'

Mr Creakle pinched my ear with ferocious playfulness.

'I'll tell you what I am,' whispered Mr Creakle, letting it go at last, with a screw at parting that brought the water into my eyes. 'I'm a Tartar.'

'A Tartar,' said the man with the wooden leg.

'Now, my young friend, you may go. Take him away.'

Tommy Traddles was the first boy who returned.

It was a happy circumstance for me. He enjoyed my placard so much, that he saved me from the embarrassment of either disclosure or concealment, by presenting me to every other boy who came back, great or small, immediately on his arrival, in this form of introduction:

'Look here! Here's a game!'

I was not considered as being formally received into the school, however, until J. Steerforth arrived.

Before this boy, who was reputed to be a great scholar, and was very good-looking, and at least half-a-dozen years my senior, I was carried as before a magistrate. He enquired, under a shed in the playground, into the particulars of my punishment, and was pleased to express his opinion that it was 'a jolly shame'; for which I became bound to him ever afterwards.

'What money have you got, Copperfield?' he said, walking aside with me when he had disposed of my affair in these terms.

I told him.

'You had better give it to me to take care of,' he said. 'At least, you can if you like. You needn't if you don't like.'

I hastened to comply with his friendly suggestion, and opening Peggotty's purse, turned it upside down into his hand.

'You belong to my bedroom, I find,' said Steerforth. 'We must make the money stretch as far as we can; I'll do the best in my power for you. I can go out when I like, and I'll smuggle the prog in.'

With these words he put the money in his pocket, and kindly told me not to make myself uneasy.

He was as good as his word. When we went upstairs to bed, he laid out the food and drink on my bed in the moonlight, saying:

'There you are, young Copperfield, and a royal spread you've got.'

I couldn't think of doing the honours of the feast. I begged him to do me the favour of presiding; and my request being seconded by the other boys who were in that room, he acceded to it, and sat upon my pillow, handing round the viands – with perfect fairness, I must say – and dispensing the currant wine in a little glass without a foot, which was his own property.

7

School began in earnest next day.

A profound impression was made upon me, I remember, by the roar of voices in the schoolroom suddenly becoming hushed as death when Mr Creakle entered after breakfast, and stood in the doorway looking round upon us like a giant in a story-book surveying his captives.

I should think there never can have been a man who enjoyed his profession more than Mr Creakle did. He had a delight in cutting at the boys, which was like the satisfaction of a craving appetite.

Steerforth continued his protection of me, and proved a very useful friend; since nobody dared to annoy one whom he honoured with his countenance. He couldn't – or at all events he didn't – defend me from Mr Creakle, who was very severe with me; but whenever I had been treated worse than usual, he always told me that I wanted a little of his pluck, and that he wouldn't have stood it himself; which I felt he intended for encouragement, and considered to be very kind of him.

There was one advantage, and only one that I know of, in Mr Creakle's severity. He found my placard in his way when he came up or down behind the form on which I sat, and wanted to make a cut at me in passing; for this reason it was soon taken off, and I saw it no more.

An accidental circumstance cemented the intimacy between Steerforth and me. It happened on one occasion, when he was doing me the honour of talking to me in the playground, that I hazarded the observation that something or somebody – I forget what now – was like something or somebody in *Peregrine Pickle*. He said nothing at the time; but when I was going to bed at night, he asked me if I had got that book.

I told him no, and explained how it was that I had read it, and all those other books of which I have made mention.

'And do you recollect them?' said Steerforth.

'Oh yes,' I replied; I had a good memory, and I believed I recollected them very well.

'Then I tell you what, young Copperfield,' said Steerforth, 'you shall tell 'em to me. I can't get to sleep very early at night, and I generally wake rather early in the morning. We'll go over 'em one after another. We'll make some regular Arabian Nights of it.'

I felt extremely flattered by this arrangement, and we commenced carrying it into execution that very evening.

What ravages I committed on my favourite authors in the course of my interpretation of them, I am not in a condition to say, and should be very unwilling to know; but I had a profound faith in them, and I had, to the best of my belief, a simple, earnest manner of narrating what I did narrate; and these qualities went a long way.

There was only one other event in this half-year, out of the daily school life, that made an impression upon me which still survives. It survives for many reasons.

One afternoon, when we were all harassed into a state of dire confusion, and Mr Creakle was laying about him dreadfully, the man with the wooden leg, whose name was Tungay, came in, and called out: 'Visitors for Copperfield!'

A few words were interchanged between him and Mr Creakle as to who the visitors were, and what room they were to be shown into; and then I, who had, according to custom, stood up on the announcement being made, and felt quite faint with astonishment, was told to go by the back stairs and get a clean frill on, before I repaired to the dining room.

These orders I obeyed, and when I got to the parlour door, and the thought came into my head that it might be my mother – I had only thought of Mr and Miss Murdstone until then – I drew back my hand from the lock, and stopped to have a sob before I went in.

At first I saw nobody; but feeling a pressure against the door, I looked round it, and there, to my amazement, were Mr Peggotty and Ham, ducking at me with their hats, and squeezing one another against the wall. I could not help laughing; but it was much more in the pleasure of seeing them, than at the appearance they made. We shook hands in a very cordial way; and I laughed and laughed, until I pulled out my pocket-handkerchief and wiped my eyes.

'Ain't he growed!' said Mr Peggotty.

They made me laugh again by laughing at each other, and then we all three laughed until I was in danger of crying again.

'Do you know how mama is, Mr Peggotty?' I said. 'And how my dear, dear, old Peggotty is?'

'Oncommon,' said Mr Peggotty.

'And little Em'ly and Mrs Gummidge?'

'Oncommon,' said Mr Peggotty.

There was a silence. Mr Peggotty, to relieve it, took two prodigious lobsters, and an enormous crab, and a large canvas bag of shrimps, out of his pockets, and piled them up in Ham's arms.

I dare say they would have said much more, if they had not been abashed by the unexpected coming in of Steerforth, who, seeing me in the corner speaking with two strangers, stopped.

'I didn't know you were here, young Copperfield!'

'Don't go, Steerforth, if you please. These are two Yarmouth boatmen – very kind, good people – who are relations of my nurse, and have come from Gravesend to see me.'

'Aye, aye?' said Steerforth, returning. 'I am glad to see them. How are you both?'

There was an ease in his manner which I still believe to have borne a kind of enchantment with it. I still believe him, in virtue of this carriage, his animal spirits, his delightful voice, his handsome face and figure, and, for aught I know, of some inborn power of attraction besides (which I think few people possess), to have carried a spell with him to which it was a natural weakness to yield, and which not many persons could withstand.

I could not but see how pleased they were with him and how they seemed to open their hearts to him in a moment.

'You must let them know at home, if you please, Mr Peggotty,' I said, 'that Mr Steerforth is very kind to me, and that I don't know what I should ever do here without him.'

'Nonsense!' said Steerforth, laughing. 'You mustn't tell them anything of the sort.'

'And if Mr Steerforth ever comes into Norfolk or Suffolk, Mr Peggotty,' I said, 'while I am here, you may depend upon it that I shall bring him to Yarmouth, if he will let me, to see your house. You never saw such a good house, Steerforth. It's made out of a boat!'

'Made out of a boat, is it?' said Steerforth. 'It's the right sort of a house for such a thorough-built boatman.'

'I thankee, sir, I thankee!' said Mr Peggotty. 'I do my endeavours in my line of life, sir.'

'The best of men can do no more, Mr Peggotty,' said Steerforth.

'I'll pound it, it's wot you do yourself, sir,' said Mr

Peggotty. 'I'm rough, sir, but I'm ready. My house ain't much for to see, sir, but it's hearty at your service if ever you should come along with Mas'r Davy to see it.

'I'm a regular Dodman, I am,' said Mr Peggotty, by which he meant snail, and this was an allusion to his being slow to go, for he had attempted to go after every sentence, and had somehow or other come back again. 'But I wish you both well and I wish you happy.'

Ham echoed this sentiment and we parted with them in the heartiest manner.

The rest of the half-year is a jumble in my recollection of the daily strife and struggle of our lives. I well remember, though, how the distant idea of the holidays, after seeming for an immense time to be a stationary speck, began to come towards us, and to grow and grow. How from counting months, we came to weeks, and then to days; the day after to-morrow, to-morrow, today, tonight – when I was inside the Yarmouth mail, and going home.

8

We arrived before day at the inn where the mail stopped, and I was shown up to a nice little bedroom, with DOLPHIN painted on the door. Mr Barkis the carrier was to call for me in the morning at nine o'clock. I got up at eight, a little giddy from the shortness of my night's rest, and was ready for him before the appointed time.

As soon as I and my box were in the cart, the lazy horse walked away with us all at his accustomed pace.

'I gave your message, Mr Barkis,' I said. 'I wrote to Peggotty.'

'Nothing come of it,' he said, looking at me sideways. 'No answer.'

'There was an answer expected, was there, Mr Barkis?' I said, opening my eyes. For this was a new light to me.

'You might tell her, if you would,' said Mr Barkis, with another slow look at me, 'that Barkis was a waitin' for a answer. Says you – what name is it?'

'Peggotty.'

'Chrisen name?' said Mr Barkis.

'Her Christian name is Clara.'

'Is it though?' said Mr Barkis.

He seemed to find an immense fund of reflection in this circumstance, and sat pondering for some time. 'Well,' he resumed at length. 'Says you, "Peggoty! Barkis is waitin' for a answer." Says she, perhaps, "Answer to what?" "Barkis is willin'," says you.'

This extremely artful suggestion Mr Barkis accompanied with a nudge of his elbow that gave me quite a stitch in my side. After that, he slouched over his horse in his usual manner and made no other reference to the subject except, half-an-hour afterwards, taking a piece of chalk from his pocket and writing up, inside the tilt of the cart, 'Clara Peggotty' – apparently as a private memorandum.

What a strange feeling it was to be going home when it was not home.

The carrier put my box down at the garden-gate, and left me. I walked along the path towards the house, glancing at the windows, and fearing at every step to see Mr Murdstone or Miss Murdstone lowering out of one of them. No face appeared, however, and I heard the sound of my mother's voice in the old parlour, when I set foot in the hall. She was singing in a low tone. I went softly into the room. She was sitting by the fire, suckling an infant, whose tiny hand she held against her neck.

I spoke to her, and she started, and cried out. But seeing me, she called me her dear Davy, her own boy! And coming half across the room to meet me, she kneeled down upon the ground and kissed me, and laid my head down on her bosom near the little creature that was nestling there, and put its hand to my lips.

I wish I had died. I wish I had died then, with that feeling in my heart! I should have been more fit for Heaven than I ever have been since.

'He is your brother,' said my mother, fondling me. 'Davy, my pretty boy! My poor child!'

Then she kissed me more and more, and clasped me round the neck. This she was doing when Peggotty came running in, and bounced down on the ground beside us, and went mad about us both for a quarter of an hour.

It seemed that I had not been expected so soon, the carrier being much before his usual time. It seemed, too, that Mr and Miss Murdstone had gone out upon a visit in the neighbourhood, and would not return before night.

I had never hoped for this. I had never thought it possible that we three could be together undisturbed, once more.

We dined together by the fireside.

While we were at table, I thought it a favourable occasion to tell Peggotty about Mr Barkis, who, before I had finished what I had to tell her, began to laugh, and throw her apron over her face.

'Peggotty,' said my mother. 'What's the matter?'

Peggotty only laughed the more, and held her apron tight

over her face when my mother tried to pull it away, and sat as if her head were in a bag.

'What are you doing, you stupid creature?' said my mother, laughing.

'Oh, drat the man!' cried Peggotty. 'He wants to marry me.'

'It would be a very good match for you – wouldn't it?' said my mother.

'Oh! I don't know,' said Peggotty. 'Don't ask me. I wouldn't have him if he was made of gold. Nor I wouldn't have anybody.'

'Then why don't you tell him so, you ridiculous thing?' said my mother.

'Tell him so,' retorted Peggotty, looking out of her apron. 'He has never said a word to me about it. He knows better. If he was to make so bold as to say a word to me, I should slap his face.'

Her own face was as red as ever I saw it, or any other face, I think; but she only covered it again, for a few moments at a time, when she was taken with a violent fit of laughter; and after two or three of those attacks, went on with her dinner.

Afterwards we sat round the fire, and talked delightfully. I told them what a hard master Mr Creakle was, and they pitied me very much. I told them what a fine fellow Steerforth was, and what a patron of mine, and Peggotty said she would walk a score of miles to see him. I took the little baby in my arms when it was awake, and nursed it lovingly. When it was asleep again, I crept close to my mother's side according to my old custom, broken now a long time, and sat with my arms embracing her waist, and my little red cheek on her shoulder, and once more felt her beautiful hair drooping over me – like an angel's wings as I used to think, I recollect – and was very happy indeed.

While I sat thus, looking at the fire, and seeing pictures in the red-hot coals, I almost believed that I had never been away; that Mr and Miss Murdstone were such pictures, and would vanish when the fire got low.

'I wonder,' said Peggotty, 'what's become of Davy's great-aunt?'

'Lor, Peggotty!' observed my mother, rousing herself from a reverie, 'what nonsense you talk! Miss Betsey is shut up in her cottage by the sea, no doubt, and will remain there. At all events, she is not likely ever to trouble us again.'

'No!' mused Peggotty. 'No, that ain't likely at all. I wonder, if she was to die, whether she'd leave Davy anything?'

'Good gracious me, Peggotty,' returned my mother, 'what a nonsensical woman you are, when you know that she took offence at the poor dear boy's ever being born at all.'

It was almost ten o'clock before we heard the sound of wheels. We all got up then; and my mother said hurriedly that, as it was so late, and Mr and Miss Murdstone approved of early hours for young people, perhaps I had better go to bed. I kissed her, and went upstairs with my candle directly, before they came in.

I felt uncomfortable about going down to breakfast in

the morning, as I had never set eyes on Mr Murdstone since the day when I committed my memorable offence. However, as it must be done, I went down and presented myself in the parlour.

He was standing before the fire with his back to it, while Miss Murdstone made the tea. He looked at me steadily as I entered, but made no sign of recognition whatever.

I went up to him, and said:

'I beg your pardon, sir, I am very sorry for what I did, and I hope you will forgive me.'

'I am glad to hear you are sorry, David,' he replied.

'How do you do, ma'am?' I said to Miss Murdstone.

'Ah, dear me!' sighed Miss Murdstone. 'How long are the holidays?'

'A month, ma'am.'

'Counting from when?'

'From today, ma'am.'

'Oh!' said Miss Murdstone. 'Then here's *one* day off.'

She kept a calendar of the holidays in this way, and every morning checked a day off in exactly the same manner.

What intolerable dulness to sit listening to the ticking of the clock; and watching Miss Murdstone's little shiny steel beads as she strung them. What walks I took alone, down muddy lanes, in the bad winter weather. What meals I had in silence and embarrassment. What evenings, when the candles came, and not daring to read an entertaining book, I pored over some hard-hearted treatise on arithmetic;

when the tables of weights and measures set themselves to tunes. What yawns and dozes I lapsed into, in spite of all my care; what answers I never got, to little observations that I rarely made; what a blank space I seemed, which everybody overlooked, and yet was in everybody's way.

Thus the holidays lagged away, until the morning came when Miss Murdstone said: 'Here's the last day off!' and gave me the closing cup of tea of the vacation.

I was not sorry to go. Again Mr Barkis appeared at the gate, and again Miss Murdstone, in her warning voice, said: 'Clara!' when my mother bent over me, to bid me farewell.

I was in the carrier's cart when I heard my mother calling to me. I looked out, and she stood at the garden-gate alone, holding her baby up in her arms for me to see.

So I saw her afterwards, in my sleep at school – a silent presence near my bed, looking at me with the same intent face, holding up her baby in her arms.

9

I pass over all that happened at school, until the anniversary of my birthday came round in March.

It was after breakfast, and we had been summoned in from the playground, when Mr Sharp entered and said:

'David Copperfield is to go into the parlour.'

I expected a hamper from Peggotty, and brightened at the order. I hurried away to the parlour; and there I found Mr Creakle, sitting at his breakfast with a cane and a newspaper before him, and Mrs Creakle with an opened letter in her hand. But no hamper.

'David Copperfield,' said Mrs Creakle, leading me to a sofa, and sitting down beside me, 'I want to speak to you very particularly. I have something to tell you, my child.'

I trembled without distinctly knowing why, and looked at her earnestly.

'I grieve to tell you that I hear this morning your mama is very ill.'

A mist rose between Mrs Creakle and me. Then I felt the burning tears run down my face. I knew all now.

'She is dead.'

There was no need to tell me so. I had already broken out into a desolate cry, and felt an orphan in the wide world.

She was very kind to me. She kept me there all day, and left me alone sometimes; and I cried, and wore myself to sleep, and awoke and cried again.

I left Salem House upon the morrow afternoon. I little thought then that I left it, never to return.

In the days before the funeral, I saw but little of Peggotty, except that, in passing up or downstairs, I always found her close to the room where my mother and her baby lay – for the child did not survive her by more than a day.

We stand around the grave. There is a solemn hush; and while we stand bareheaded, I hear the voice of the clergyman, sounding remote in the open air, and yet distinct and plain, saying: 'I am the Resurrection and the Life, saith the Lord.'

It is over, and the earth is filled in, and we turn to come away.

10

The first act of business Miss Murdstone performed when the day of the solemnity was over, was to give Peggotty a month's warning.

As to me or my future, not a word was said. Happy they would have been, I dare say, if they could have dismissed me at a month's warning too.

'And what do you mean to do, Peggotty?' I said.

'I'm a-going, Davy, to my brother's first, for another fort-night's visit – just till I have had time to look about me, and get to be something like myself again. Now, I have been thinking that perhaps, as they don't want you here at present, you might be let to go along with me.'

Peggotty, with a boldness that amazed me, broached the topic with Miss Murdstone on the spot.

'The boy will be idle there,' said Miss Murdstone, 'but it is of paramount importance that my brother should not be disturbed or made uncomfortable. I suppose I had better say yes.'

Permission given, it was never retracted, and when the month was out, Peggotty and I were ready to depart.

Mr Barkis came into the house for Peggotty's boxes. Peggotty was naturally in low spirits at leaving what had been her home so many years, and she got into the cart, and sat in it with her handkerchief at her eyes.

So long as she remained in this condition, Mr Barkis gave no sign of life whatever. But when she began to look about her, and to speak to me, he nodded his head and grinned several times.

'Peggotty is quite comfortable now, Mr Barkis,' I remarked, for his satisfaction.

'Is she though?' said Mr Barkis.

After reflecting about it, with a sagacious air, Mr Barkis eyed her, and said:

'*Are* you pretty comfortable?'

Peggotty laughed, and answered in the affirmative.

'But really and truly, you know. Are you?' growled Mr Barkis, sliding nearer to her on the seat, and nudging her with his elbow. 'Are you? Really and truly pretty comfortable? Are you? Eh?'

At each of these inquiries Mr Barkis shuffled nearer to her, and gave her another nudge; so that at last we were all crowded together in the left-hand corner of the cart, and I was so squeezed that I could hardly bear it.

At length, I got up, and standing on the foot-board, pretended to look at the prospect.

Mr Peggotty and Ham waited for us at the old place. They each took one of Peggotty's trunks, and we were going away, when Mr Barkis solemnly made a sign to me with his forefinger to come under an archway.

'I say,' growled Mr Barkis, 'it was all right.'

I looked up into his face, and answered, with an attempt to be very profound: 'Oh!'

'It didn't come to an end there,' said Mr Barkis, nodding confidentially. 'It was all right.'

As we were going along, Peggoty asked me what he had said; and I told her he had said it was all right.

'Like his impudence,' said Peggotty. 'Davy dear, what should you think if I was to think of being married?'

'To Mr Barkis, Peggotty?'

'Yes,' said Peggotty.

'I should think it would be a very good thing indeed. For then you know, Peggotty, you would always have the horse and cart to bring you over to see me, and could come for nothing, and be sure of coming.'

'The sense of the dear!' cried Peggotty. 'What have I been thinking of, this month back! Yes, my precious: and I think I should be more independent altogether, you see; let alone my working with a better heart in my own house, than I could in anybody else's now. I don't know what I might be fit for, now, as a servant to a stranger.'

Mr Peggotty's cottage looked just the same, except that it may, perhaps, have shrunk a little in my eyes; and Mrs

Gummidge was waiting at the door as if she had stood there ever since.

The days passed pretty much as they had passed before, except – and it was a great exception – that little Em'ly and I seldom wandered on the beach now. She had tasks to learn, and needle-work to do; and was absent during a great part of each day.

On the very first evening of our arrival, Mr Barkis appeared in an exceedingly vacant and awkward condition, and with a bundle of oranges tied up in a handkerchief. As he made no allusion of any kind to this property, he was supposed to have left it behind him by accident when he went away; until Ham, running after him to restore it, came back with the information that it was intended for Peggotty.

After that occasion he appeared every evening at exactly the same hour, and always with a little bundle, to which he never alluded, and which he regularly put behind the door and left there. These offerings of affection were of a most various and eccentric description. Among them I remember a double set of pigs' trotters, a huge pincushion, half a bushel or so of apples, a pair of jet earrings, some Spanish onions, a box of dominoes, a canary bird and cage, and a leg of pickled pork.

Mr Barkis's wooing, as I remember it, was altogether of a peculiar kind. He very seldom said anything; but would sit by the fire in very much the same attitude as he sat in his cart, and stare heavily at Peggotty, who was opposite.

At length, when the term of my visit was nearly expired, it was given out that Peggotty and Mr Barkis were going to make a day's holiday together, and that little Em'ly and I were to accompany them. I had but a broken sleep the night before, in anticipation of the pleasure of a whole day with Em'ly. We were all astir betimes in the morning; and while we were yet at breakfast, Mr Barkis appeared in the distance, driving a chaise-cart towards the object of his affections.

Peggotty was dressed as usual, in her neat and quiet mourning; but Mr Barkis bloomed in a new blue coat.

Away we went, however, on our holiday excursion; and the first thing we did was to stop at a church, where Mr Barkis tied the horse to some rails, and went in with Peggotty, leaving little Em'ly and me alone in the chaise. I took that occasion to put my arm round Em'ly's waist, and she allowed me to kiss her.

Mr Barkis and Peggotty were a good while in the church, but came out at last, and then we drove away into the country. As we were going along, Mr Barkis turned to me, and said, with a wink:

'What name was it as I wrote up in the cart?'

'Clara Peggotty,' I answered.

'What name would it be as I should write up now?'

'Clara Peggotty, again?' I suggested.

'Clara Peggotty BARKIS!' he returned, and burst into a roar of laughter that shook the chaise.

In a word, they were married, and had gone into the

church for no other purpose. Peggotty was resolved that it should be quietly done; and the clerk had given her away, and there had been no witnesses of the ceremony. She was a little confused when Mr Barkis made this abrupt announcement of their union, and could not hug me enough in token of her unimpaired affection; but she soon became herself again, and said that she was very glad it was over.

We drove to a little inn in a by-road, where we were expected, and where we had a very comfortable dinner, and passed the day with great satisfaction. We got into the chaise again soon after dark, and drove cosily back.

We came to the old boat again in good time, and there Mr and Mrs Barkis bade us good-bye, and drove away snugly to their own home.

With morning came Peggotty who called to me, as usual, under my window as if Mr Barkis the carrier had been from the first to last a dream too. After breakfast she took me to her own home, and a beautiful little home it was.

I took leave of Mr Peggotty, and Ham, and Mrs Gummidge, and little Em'ly, that day and passed the night at Peggotty's in a little room in the roof which was to be always mine, Peggotty said, and should always be kept for me in exactly the same state.

'Young or old, Davy dear, as long as I am alive and have this house over my head, you shall find it as if I expected you here directly.'

In the morning I went home with herself and Mr Barkis in the cart. They left me at the gate, not easily or lightly; and it was strange to see the cart go on, taking Peggotty away, and leaving me under the old elm-trees looking at the house, in which there was no face to look on mine with love or liking any more.

And now I fell into a stage of neglect – apart from all friendly notice, apart from the society of all other boys of my own age. Day after day, week after week, month after month, I was coldly neglected.

When Mr and Miss Murdstone were at home, I took my meals with them; in their absence, I ate and drank by myself. At all times I lounged about the house and neighbourhood quite disregarded, except that they were jealous of my making any friends.

One day after breakfast, Mr Murdstone called me. A gentleman with his hands in his pockets stood looking out of the window.

'David,' said Mr Murdstone. 'You have heard the "counting-house" mentioned sometimes.'

'The counting-house, sir?'

'Of Murdstone and Grinby, in the wine trade,' he replied. 'This is Mr Quinion who manages that business.'

I glanced at the latter deferentially as he stood looking out of the window.

'Mr Quinion suggests that it gives employment to some other boys, and that he sees no reason why it shouldn't, on the same terms, give employment to you. Those terms are, that you will earn enough for yourself to provide for your eating and drinking, and pocket-money. Your lodging (which I have arranged for) will be paid by me. So you are now going to London, David, with Mr Quinion, to begin the world on your own account.'

Behold me, on the morrow, with my little worldly all before me in a small trunk, sitting, a lone lorn child (as Mrs Gummidge might have said), in the post-chaise that was carrying Mr Quinion to the London coach at Yarmouth!

11

Murdstone and Grinby's warehouse was at the waterside down in Blackfriars. Murdstone and Grinby's trade was the supply of wines and spirits to certain packet ships. A great many empty bottles were one of the consequences of this traffic, and certain men and boys were employed to examine them against the light, and reject those that were flawed, and to rinse and wash them. When the empty bottles ran short, there were labels to be pasted on full ones, or corks to be fitted to them, or seals to be put upon the corks, or finished bottles to be packed in casks. All this work was my work, and of the boys employed upon it I was one.

No words can express the secret agony of my soul at the sense I had of being utterly without hope now; of the shame I felt in my position.

The counting-house clock was at half-past twelve, and there was general preparation for going to dinner, when Mr Quinion tapped at the counting-house window, and beckoned me to go in.

I went in, and found there a stoutish, middle-aged person, in a brown surtout and black tights and shoes, with no more hair upon his head (which was a large one, and very shining) than there is upon an egg, and with a very extensive face, which he turned full upon me. He carried a jaunty sort of a stick, with a large pair of rusty tassels to it; and a quizzing-glass hung outside his coat.

'This,' said Mr Quinion, in allusion to myself, 'is he.'

'This,' said the stranger, 'is Master Copperfield. I hope I see you well, sir?'

I said I was very well, and hoped he was.

'I am,' said the stranger, 'thank Heaven, quite well. I have received a letter from Mr Murdstone, in which he mentions that he would desire me to receive into an apartment in the rear of my house, which is at present unoccupied . . .' and the stranger waved his hand.

'This is Mr Micawber,' said Mr Quinion to me.

'That,' said the stranger, 'is my name, and I shall be happy to call this evening, and convey you thither.'

I thanked him with all my heart, for it was friendly in him to offer to take that trouble.

'At what hour,' said Mr Micawber, 'shall I . . .?'

'At about eight,' said Mr Quinion.

'At about eight,' said Mr Micawber. 'I beg to wish you good day, Mr Quinion. I will no longer intrude.'

So he put on his hat, and went out with his cane under his arm – very upright, and humming a tune.

At the appointed time in the evening Mr Micawber re-appeared, and we walked to our house, as I suppose I must now call it, together; Mr Micawber impressing the name of the streets, and the shapes of corner houses upon me, as we went along, that I might find my way back easily in the morning.

Arrived at this house in Windsor Terrace, he presented me to Mrs Micawber, a thin, faded lady, not at all young, who was sitting in the parlour with a baby at her breast.

This baby was one of twins; and I may remark here that I hardly ever, in all my experience of the family, saw both the twins detached from Mrs Micawber at the same time. One of them was always taking refreshment.

There were two other children: Master Micawber, aged about four, and Miss Micawber, aged about three. These, and a dark-complexioned young woman, with a habit of snorting, who was servant to the family, and informed me, before half-an-hour had expired, that she was 'a Orfling', and came from St Luke's workhouse, in the neighbourhood, completed the establishment.

'I never thought,' said Mrs Micawber, when she came up, twin and all, to show me my apartment, and sat down to take breath, 'before I was married, when I lived with papa and mama, that I should ever find it necessary to take a lodger. But Mr Micawber being in difficulties, all considerations of private feeling must give way.'

I said: 'Yes, ma'am.'

'Mr Micawber's difficulties are almost overwhelming just at present,' said Mrs Micawber. 'If Mr Micawber's creditors *will not* give him time, they must take the consequences. Blood cannot be obtained from a stone.'

Mr Micawber's difficulties were an addition to the distressed state of my mind. In my forlorn state I became quite attached to the family, and used to walk about, busy with Mrs Micawber's calculations of ways and means, and heavy with the weight of Mr Micawber's debts.

'Master Copperfield,' said Mrs Micawber one evening, 'I make no stranger of you, and therefore do not hesitate to say that with the exception of the heel of a Dutch cheese – which is not adapted to the wants of a young family – there is nothing to eat in the house.'

'Dear me!' I said, in great concern.

I had two or three shillings of my week's money in my pocket – from which I presume that it must have been on a Wednesday night when we held this conversation – and I hastily produced them, and with heartfelt emotion begged Mrs Micawber to accept of them as a loan. But that lady, kissing me, and making me put them back in my pocket, replied that she couldn't think of it.

'No, my dear Master Copperfield,' she said, 'far be it from my thoughts! But you can render me another kind of service, if you will; and a service I will thankfully accept of.'

I begged Mrs Micawber to name it.

'I have parted with the plate myself,' said Mrs Micawber.

'Six tea, two salt, and a pair of sugars. But there are still a few trifles that we could part with. Mr Micawber's feelings would never allow *him* to dispose of them; and Clickett' – this was the girl from the workhouse – 'being of a vulgar mind, would take painful liberties if so much confidence was reposed in her. Master Copperfield, if I might ask you . . .'

I understood Mrs Micawber now, and begged her to make use of me to any extent. I began to dispose of the more portable articles of property that very evening; and went out on a similar expedition almost every morning, before I went to Murdstone and Grinby's.

At last Mr Micawber's difficulties came to a crisis, and he was arrested early one morning and carried over to the King's Bench Prison in the Borough. He told me, as he went out of the house, that the God of day had now gone down upon him – and I really thought his heart was broken, and mine too. But I heard, afterwards, that he was seen to play a lively game of skittles, before noon.

12

In due time, Mr Micawber's petition was ripe for hearing; and that gentleman was ordered to be discharged under the Act, to my great joy.

I said to Mrs Micawber:

'May I ask, ma'am, what you and Mr Micawber intend to do, now that Mr Micawber is out of his difficulties, and at liberty?'

'My family,' said Mrs Micawber, 'are of opinion that Mr Micawber should quit London, and exert his talents in the country. Mr Micawber is a man of great talent, Master Copperfield.'

I said I was sure of that.

'It is their wish that Mr Micawber should go down to Plymouth. They think it indispensable that he should be upon the spot – in case of anything turning up.'

'And do you go too, ma'am?'

The events of the day had made Mrs Micawber hysterical.

'I will never desert Mr Micawber. I will never do it! It's of no use asking me!'

I felt quite uncomfortable – as if Mrs Micawber supposed I had asked her to do anything of the sort!

'He is the parent of my children!' cried Mrs Micawber. 'He is the father of my twins! He is the husband of my affections, and I ne – ver – will – desert Mr Micawber!'

Through all the confusion and lowness of spirits, I plainly discerned that Mr and Mrs Micawber and their family were going away from London, and that a parting between us was near at hand.

During the remaining term of our residence under the same roof, I passed my evenings with Mr and Mrs Micawber; and I think we became fonder of one another as the time went on. On the last Sunday, they invited me to dinner and we had a very pleasant day, though we were all in a tender state about our approaching separation.

'My dear young friend,' said Mr Micawber. 'Until something turns up (which I am, I may say, hourly expecting), I have nothing to bestow but advice. My advice is, never do to-morrow what you can do today. Procrastination is the thief of time. Collar him!'

'My poor papa's maxim,' observed Mrs Micawber.

'My other piece of advice, Copperfield, you know. Annual income twenty pounds, annual expenditure nineteen nineteen and six, result happiness. Annual income twenty pounds, annual expenditure twenty pounds ought and six, result misery. The blossom is blighted, the leaf is withered, the God of day goes down upon the dreary scene, and – and in short you are for ever flawed. As I am!'

To make his example the more impressive, Mr Micawber drank a glass of punch with an air of great enjoyment and satisfaction, and whistled the College Hornpipe.

I did not fail to assure him that I would store these precepts in my mind, though indeed I had no need to do so, for at the time they affected me visibly.

Next morning I met the whole family at the coach office and saw them, with a desolate heart, take their places outside at the back.

As Mrs Micawber sat at the back of the coach with the children, and I stood in the road looking wistfully at them, she beckoned to me to climb up, put her arm round my neck, and gave me just such a kiss as she might have given to her own boy. I had barely time to get down again before the coach started, and I could hardly see the family for the handkerchiefs they waved. It was gone in a minute.

I went to begin my weary day at Murdstone and Grinby's. But with no intention of passing many more weary days there. No. I had resolved to run away. To go, by some means or other, down into the country, to the only relation I had in the world, and to tell my story to my aunt, Miss Betsey.

As I did not even know where Miss Betsey lived, I wrote a long letter to Peggotty, and asked her.

Peggotty's answer soon arrived and was, as usual, full of affectionate devotion. She told me that Miss Betsey lived near Dover but whether at Dover itself, at Hythe, Sandgate, or Folkestone, she could not say. One of our men, however, informing me on my asking him about these places, that they were all close together, I deemed this enough for my object, and resolved to set out at the end of that week.

13

I will not dwell on the circumstances of my journey beyond recording that I walked every step of the way, and arrived at Miss Betsey Trotwood's house in a woeful condition. My shirt and trousers, stained with heat, dew, grass, and the Kentish soil on which I had slept, might have frightened the birds from my aunt's garden, as I stood at the gate. My hair had known no comb or brush since I left London. My face, neck, and hands, from unaccustomed exposure to the air and sun, were burnt to a berry-brown. From head to foot I was powdered almost as white with chalk and dust as if I had come out of a lime-kiln.

I was thinking how I had best proceed, when there came out of the house a lady with her handkerchief tied over her cap, and a pair of gardening gloves on her hands, wearing a gardening pocket like a toll-man's apron, and carrying a great knife. I knew her immediately to be Miss Betsey, for she came stalking out of the house exactly as my poor mother had so often described her stalking up our garden.

'Go away!' said Miss Betsey, shaking her head, and

making a distant chop in the air with her knife. 'Go along! No boys here!'

Without a scrap of courage, but with a great deal of desperation, I went softly in and stood beside her, touching her with my finger.

'If you please, aunt.'

'Eh?' exclaimed Miss Betsey.

'If you please, aunt, I am your nephew.'

'Oh, Lord!' said my aunt. And sat flat down in the garden-path.

'I am David Copperfield, of Blunderstone, in Suffolk – where you came, on the night when I was born, and saw my dear mama. I have been very unhappy since she died. I have been slighted, and taught nothing, and thrown upon myself, and put to work not fit for me. It made me run away to you. I have walked all the way, and have never slept in a bed since I began the journey.'

Here my self-support gave way all at once; and I broke into a passion of crying, which I suppose had been pent up within me all the week.

My aunt got up in a great hurry, collared me, took me into the parlour and put me on the sofa, with a shawl under my head. Then, sitting herself down behind a green fan or screen, so that I could not see her face, ejaculated at intervals:

'Mercy on us!'

After a time she rang the bell.

'Janet,' said my aunt, when her servant came in. 'Go upstairs, give my compliments to Mr Dick, and say I wish to speak to him.'

My aunt, with her hands behind her, walked up and down the room, until a florid, pleasant-looking gentleman with a grey head came in.

'Mr Dick,' said my aunt, 'you have heard me mention David Copperfield? Well, this is his boy – his son.'

'His son?' said Mr Dick. 'David's son? Indeed!'

'Yes,' pursued my aunt, 'and he has done a pretty piece of business. He has run away. Ah! His sister, Betsey Trotwood, would never have run away.'

My aunt shook her head firmly, confident in the character and behaviour of the girl who never was born.

'Now, here you see young David Copperfield, and the question I put to you is, what shall I do with him?'

'What shall you do with him?' said Mr Dick, feebly, scratching his head. 'Why, if I was you,' said Mr Dick, considering, 'I should wash him!'

'Janet,' said my aunt, turning round with a quiet triumph, 'Mr Dick sets us all right. Heat the bath!'

Janet had gone away to get the bath ready, when my aunt, to my great alarm, became in one moment rigid with indignation, and had hardly voice to cry out:

'Janet! Donkeys!'

Upon which, Janet came running up the stairs as if the house were in flames, darted out on a little piece of green in front, and warned off two saddle-donkeys, lady-ridden, that had presumed to set hoof upon it; while my aunt, rushing out of the house, seized the bridle of a third animal laden with a bestriding child, turned him, let him forth from those sacred precincts, and boxed the ears of the unlucky urchin in attendance who had dared to profane that hallowed ground.

To this hour I don't know whether my aunt had any lawful right of way over that patch of green; but she had settled it in her own mind that she had, and it was all the same to her. The one great outrage of her life, demanding to be constantly avenged, was the passage of a donkey over that immaculate spot.

In whatever occupation she was engaged, however interesting to her the conversation in which she was taking part, a donkey turned the current of her ideas in a moment, and she was upon him straight. There were three alarms before my bath was ready; and on the occasion of the last and most desperate of all, I saw my aunt engage, single-handed, with a sandy-headed lad of fifteen, and bump his sandy head against her own gate, before he seemed to comprehend what was the matter.

The bath was a great comfort, and after tea we sat at the window – on the look-out, as I imagined, from my aunt's sharp expression of face, for more invaders – until dusk, when Janet set candles, and a back-gammon board, on the table, and pulled down the blinds.

'Now, Mr Dick,' said my aunt, 'I am going to ask you another question. Look at this child.'

'David's son?' said Mr Dick, with an attentive, puzzled face.

'Exactly so,' returned my aunt. 'What would you do with him, now?'

'Oh!' said Mr Dick. 'Yes. Do with . . . I should put him to bed.'

'Janet!' cried my aunt, with the same complacent triumph that I had remarked before. 'Mr Dick sets us all right. If the bed is ready, we'll take him up to it.'

14

On going down in the morning, I found my aunt musing profoundly over the breakfast table.

'Hallo!' said my aunt, after a long time. 'I have written to him.'

'To . . .?'

'To your step-father,' said my aunt. 'I have sent him a letter that I'll trouble him to attend to, or he and I will fall out.'

'Shall I – be – given up to him?' I faltered.

'I don't know,' said my aunt. 'We shall see.'

My spirits sank under these words, and I became very downcast and heavy of heart.

'I wish you'd go upstairs,' said my aunt, as she threaded her needle, 'and give my compliments to Mr Dick, and I'll be glad to know how he gets on with his Memorial.'

I rose with all alacrity and went upstairs with my message. I found him driving at it with a long pen, and his head almost laid upon the paper. He was so intent upon it that I had ample leisure to observe the large paper kite in a corner, the confusion of bundles of manuscript, the number of pens, and, above all, the quantity of ink, before he observed my being present.

'Do you recollect the date,' said Mr Dick, taking up his pen to note it down, 'when King Charles the First had his head cut off?'

I said I believed it happened in the year sixteen hundred and forty-nine.

'Well,' returned Mr Dick, scratching his ear with his pen, and looking dubiously at me. 'If it was so long ago, how could the people about him have put the trouble out of *his* head into *mine*?'

I was going away, when he directed my attention to the kite.

'What do you think of that for a kite?' he said.

I answered that it was a beautiful one. I should think it must have been as much as seven feet high.

'I made it. We'll go and fly it, you and I,' said Mr Dick. 'Do you see this?'

He showed me that it was covered with manuscript, very closely and laboriously written; but so plainly, that as I looked along the lines, I thought I saw some allusion to King Charles the First's head again, in one or two places.

The anxiety I underwent, in the interval which necessarily elapsed before a reply could be received to my aunt's letter to Mr Murdstone, was extreme; but I made an endeavour to suppress it, and to be as agreeable as I could in a quiet way, both to my aunt and Mr Dick.

At length the reply from Mr Murdstone came, and my aunt informed me, to my infinite terror, that he was coming to speak to her himself on the next day. On the next day, my aunt sat at work in the window, and I sat by, with my thoughts running astray on all possible and impossible results of Mr Murdstone's visit, until pretty late in the afternoon.

Our dinner had been indefinitely postponed; but it was growing so late, that my aunt had ordered it to be got ready, when she gave a sudden alarm of donkeys, and to my consternation and amazement, I beheld Miss Murdstone, on a side-saddle, ride deliberately over the sacred piece of green, and stop in front of the house, looking about her.

'Go along with you!' cried my aunt, shaking her head and her fist at the window. 'You have no business there. How dare you trespass? Go along! Oh! you bold-faced thing!'

I seized the opportunity to inform her who it was; and that the gentleman now coming near the offender was Mr Murdstone himself.

'I don't care who it is!' cried my aunt, still shaking her head and gesticulating anything but welcome from the bow-window. 'I won't be trespassed upon. I won't allow it. Go away! Janet, turn him round. Lead him off!' and I saw, from behind my aunt, a sort of hurried battle-piece, in which the donkey stood resisting everybody, with all his four legs planted different ways, while Janet tried to pull him round by the bridle, Mr Murdstone tried to lead him on, Miss Murdstone struck at Janet with a parasol, and several boys, who had come to see the engagement, shouted vigorously.

'Shall I go away, aunt?' I asked, trembling.

'No, sir,' said my aunt. 'Certainly not!'

With which she pushed me into a corner near her, and fenced me in with a chair, as if it were a prison or a bar of justice. This position I continued to occupy during the whole interview, and from it I now saw Mr and Miss Murdstone enter the room.

'Oh!' said my aunt, 'I was not aware at first to whom I had the pleasure of objecting. But I don't allow anybody to ride over that turf. I make no exceptions. I don't allow anybody to do it.'

'Your regulation is rather awkward to strangers,' said Miss Murdstone.

'Is it!' said my aunt.

Mr Murdstone seemed afraid of a renewal of hostilities, and interposing began:

'Miss Trotwood!'

'I beg your pardon,' observed my aunt, with a keen look. 'You are the Mr Murdstone who married the widow of my late nephew, David Copperfield, of Blunderstone?'

'I am,' said Mr Murdstone.

'You'll excuse my saying, sir,' returned my aunt, 'that I think it would have been a much better and happier thing if you had left that poor child alone.'

'I so far agree with what Miss Trotwood has remarked,' observed Miss Murdstone, bridling, 'that I consider our lamented Clara to have been, in all essential matters, a mere child.'

My aunt rang the bell.

'Janet, my compliments to Mr Dick, and beg him to come down.'

Until he came, my aunt sat perfectly upright and stiff, frowning at the wall. When he came, my aunt performed the ceremony of introduction.

'Mr Dick. An old and intimate friend. On whose judgement,' said my aunt, with emphasis, as an admonition to Mr Dick, who was biting his forefinger and looking rather foolish, 'I rely.'

Mr Dick took his finger out of his mouth, on this hint, and stood among the group, with a grave and attentive expression of face. My aunt inclined her head to Mr Murdstone, who began:

'Miss Trotwood: on the receipt of your letter, I considered it an act of respect to answer it in person, however inconvenient the journey. This unhappy boy, Miss Trotwood, has been the occasion of much domestic trouble and uneasiness; both during the lifetime of my late dear wife, and since. He has a sullen, rebellious spirit; a violent temper; and an untoward, intractable disposition. Both my sister and myself have endeavoured to correct his vices, but ineffectually.'

'It can hardly be necessary for me to confirm anything

stated by my brother,' said Miss Murdstone; 'but I beg to observe, that, of all the boys in the world, I believe this is the worst boy.'

'Strong!' said my aunt, shortly.

'I have my own opinions,' resumed Mr Murdstone, whose face darkened more and more, the more he and my aunt observed each other, which they did very narrowly, 'as to the best mode of bringing him up. It is enough that I place this boy under the eye of a friend of my own, in a respectable business; that it does not please him; that he runs away from it, makes himself a common vagabond about the country, and comes here to appeal to you, Miss Trotwood.'

'About this respectable business,' said my aunt. 'If he had been your own boy, you would have put him to it just the same, I suppose?'

'If he had been my brother's own boy,' returned Miss Murdstone, 'his character, I trust, would have been altogether different.'

'Did the poor child's annuity die with her?' said my aunt. 'It did.'

'And there was no settlement of the little property upon her boy?'

'It had been left to her, unconditionally, by her first husband,' Mr Murdstone began, when my aunt caught him up.

'Good Lord, man, of course it was left to her unconditionally. But when she married again – when she took that most disastrous step of marrying you, in short,' said my aunt, 'to be plain – did no one put in a word for the boy at that time?'

'My late wife loved her second husband, ma'am,' said Mr Murdstone, 'and trusted implicitly in him.'

'Your late wife, sir, was a most unworldly, most unhappy, most unfortunate baby,' returned my aunt, shaking her head at him. 'That's what *she* was. And now, what have you got to say next?'

'Merely this, Miss Trotwood,' he returned. 'I am here to take David back – to take him back unconditionally, to dispose of him as I think proper, and to deal with him as I think right. I am not here to make any promise, or give any pledge to anybody. Is he ready to go? If he is not, my doors are shut against him henceforth, and yours, I take it for granted, are open to him.'

'And what does the boy say?' said my aunt. 'Are you ready to go, David?'

I answered no, and entreated her not to let me go. I said that neither Mr nor Miss Murdstone had ever liked me, or had ever been kind to me. And I begged and prayed my aunt to befriend and protect me, for my father's sake.

'Mr Dick,' said my aunt. 'What shall I do with this child?'

Mr Dick considered, hesitated, brightened, and rejoined: 'Have him measured for a suit of clothes directly.'

'Mr Dick,' said my aunt triumphantly, 'give me your hand, for your common sense is invaluable.' Having shaken it with great cordiality, she pulled me towards her and said to Mr Murdstone:

'I'll take my chance with the boy. Do you think I don't know what kind of life you must have led that poor, unhappy, misdirected baby?'

'I never heard anything like this person in my life!' exclaimed Miss Murdstone.

Miss Betsey, without taking the least notice of the interruption, continued to address herself to Mr Murdstone, shaking her finger at him.

'You broke her heart. There is the truth for your comfort, however you like it. And you and your instruments may make the most of it.'

'Allow me to enquire, Miss Trotwood,' interposed Miss Murdstone, 'whom you are pleased to call my brother's instruments?'

'Good day, sir,' said my aunt, 'and good-bye! Good day to you too, ma'am,' said my aunt, turning suddenly upon his sister. 'Let me see you ride a donkey over *my* green again, and as sure as you have a head upon your shoulders, I'll knock your bonnet off, and tread upon it!'

It would require a painter, and no common painter too, to depict my aunt's face as she delivered herself of this very unexpected sentiment, and Miss Murdstone's face as she heard it. Miss Murdstone, without a word in answer, put her arm through her brother's, and walked haughtily out of the cottage.

My aunt's face gradually relaxed, and became so pleasant, that I was emboldened to kiss and thank her; which I did with great heartiness, and with both my arms clasped round her neck. I then shook hands with Mr Dick, who shook hands with me a great many times, and hailed this happy close of the proceedings with repeated bursts of laughter.

'You'll consider yourself guardian, jointly with me, of this child, Mr Dick,' said my aunt.

'I shall be delighted,' said Mr Dick, 'to be the guardian of David's son.'

'Very good,' returned my aunt, '*that's* settled. I have been thinking, do you know, Mr Dick, that I might call him Trotwood Copperfield.'

'Yes, to be sure. Yes. Trotwood Copperfield,' said Mr Dick.

My aunt took so kindly to the notion, that some ready-made clothes, which were purchased for me that afternoon, were marked 'Trotwood Copperfield', in her own handwriting, and in indelible marking-ink. Other clothes which were ordered to be made for me (a complete outfit was bespoke that afternoon) were to be marked in the same way.

Thus I began my new life, in a new name, and with everything new about me.

15

'Trot,' said my aunt one evening, when the back-gammon board was placed as usual for herself and Mr Dick, 'should you like to go to school at Canterbury?'

I replied that I should like it very much, as it was so near here.

'Good,' said my aunt. 'Janet, hire the grey pony and chaise to-morrow morning at ten o'clock, and pack up Master Trotwood's clothes tonight.'

In the morning my aunt, who was perfectly indifferent to public opinion, drove the grey pony through Dover, sitting high and stiff like a state coachman. When he came into the country road, she looked at me and asked me whether I was happy?

'Very happy indeed, thank you, aunt,' I said.

She was much gratified, and patted me on the head with her whip.

'Is it a large school, aunt?'

'Why, I don't know. We are going to Mr Wickfield's first.'

'Does *he* keep a school?' I asked.

'No, Trot,' said my aunt. 'He keeps an office.'

We conversed on other subjects until we came to Canterbury, where at length we stopped before a very old house bulging out over the road. The low arched door opened, and a red-haired person – a youth of fifteen, as I take it now, but looking much older – came out. He was high-shouldered and bony; dressed in decent black, with a white wisp of a neckcloth; buttoned up to the throat; and had a long, lank, skeleton hand, which particularly attracted my attention, as he stood at the pony's head, rubbing his chin with it, and looking up at us in the chaise.

'Is Mr Wickfield at home, Uriah Heep?' said my aunt.

'Mr Wickfield's at home, ma'am,' said Uriah Heep, 'if you'll please to walk in there,' – pointing with his long hand to the room he meant.

Mr Wickfield's hair was quite white and he had a very agreeable face.

'Well, Miss Trotwood,' he said, 'what wind blows you here? Not an ill wind, I hope?'

'No,' replied my aunt. 'I have not come for any law. This is my nephew.'

'Wasn't aware that you had one, Miss Trotwood,' said Mr Wickfield.

'I have adopted him,' said my aunt, with a wave of her hand, importing that his knowledge and his ignorance were all one to her, 'and I have brought him here, to put him to a school where he may be thoroughly well taught, and well treated. Now tell me where that school is, and what it is, and all about it.'

'At the best we have,' said Mr Wickfield, considering, 'your nephew couldn't board just now.'

'But he could board somewhere else, I suppose?' suggested my aunt.

Mr Wickfield thought I could.

'Leave your nephew here, for the present. He won't disturb me at all. It's a capital house for study. As quiet as a monastery and almost as roomy. Leave him here.'

My aunt evidently liked the offer, though she was delicate of accepting it.

'Come, Miss Trotwood,' said Mr Wickfield. 'You may pay for him, if you like. We won't be hard about terms, but you shall pay if you will.'

'On that understanding,' said my aunt, 'though it doesn't lessen the real obligation, I shall be very glad to leave him.'

'Then come and see my little housekeeper,' said Mr Wickfield.

We accordingly went up a wonderful old staircase. Mr Wickfield tapped at a door in the corner of the panelled wall, and a girl of about my own age came quickly out and kissed him. Although her face was quite bright and happy, there was a tranquillity about it, and about her – a quiet, good, calm spirit – that I never have forgotten, that I shall never forget.

This was his little housekeeper, his daughter Agnes, Mr Wickfield said. When I heard how he said it, and saw how he held her hand, I guessed what the one motive of his life was.

16

Next morning, after breakfast, I entered on school life again. I went, accompanied by Mr Wickfield, to the scene of my future studies – a grave building in a courtyard, with a learned air about it that seemed very well suited to the stray rooks and jackdaws who came down from the Cathedral towers to walk with a clerkly bearing on the grass-plot – and was introduced to my new master, Doctor Strong.

Doctor Strong was in his library, with his clothes not particularly well brushed, and his hair not particularly well combed. But, sitting at work, not far from Doctor Strong, was a very pretty young lady – whom he called Annie, and who was his daughter, I supposed. When we were going out to the schoolroom, I was much surprised to hear Mr Wickfield, in bidding her good morning, address her as 'Mrs Strong'.

That evening after dinner, Agnes having left us, I gave Mr Wickfield my hand, preparatory to going away myself. But he checked me and said:

'Should you like to stay with us, Trotwood, or to go elsewhere?'

'To stay,' I answered quickly. 'I am so glad to be here.'

'That's a fine fellow!' said Mr Wickfield. 'As long as you're glad to be here, you shall stay here.'

He shook hands with me upon it, and told me that when I had anything to do at night after Agnes had left us, or when I wished to read for my own pleasure, I was free to come down to his room and to sit with him. I thanked him for his consideration; and, as he went down soon afterwards, and I was not tired, went down too, with a book in my hand, to avail myself for half-an-hour of his permission.

But seeing a light in the little round office, I went in there instead. I found Uriah reading a great fat book.

'You are working late tonight, Uriah,' I said.

'I am not doing office-work, Master Copperfield,' said Uriah. 'I am improving my legal knowledge. I am going through Tidd's Practice.'

'I suppose you are quite a great lawyer?' I said.

'Me, Master Copperfield?' said Uriah, 'Oh, no! I'm a very umble person. My mother is likewise a very umble person. We live in a numble abode, Master Copperfield, but have much to be thankful for.'

I asked Uriah if he had been with Mr Wickfield long?

'I have been with him going on four year, Master Copperfield,' said Uriah; shutting up his book. 'Since a year after my father's death. How much have I to be thankful for, in

Mr Wickfield's kind intention to give me my articles, which would otherwise not lay within the umble means of mother and self!'

'Then, when your articled time is over, you'll be a regular lawyer, I suppose?'

'With the blessing of Providence, Master Copperfield.'

'Perhaps you'll be a partner in Mr Wickfield's business, one of these days,' I said, to make myself agreeable; 'and it will be Wickfield and Heep, or Heep late Wickfield.'

'Oh, no, Master Copperfield,' returned Uriah, shaking his head, 'I am much too umble for that!'

Doctor Strong's was an excellent school; as different from Mr Creakle's as good is from evil. It was very gravely and decorously ordered, and on a sound system; with an appeal, in everything, to the honour and good faith of the boys. We all felt that we had a part in the management of the place, and in sustaining its character and dignity. Hence, we soon became warmly attached to it – I am sure I did for one, and I never knew, in all my time, any other boy being otherwise – and learnt with good will, desiring to do it credit. We had noble games out of hours, and plenty of liberty; but even then, as I remember, we were well spoken of in the town, and rarely did any disgrace, by our appearance or manner, to the reputation of Doctor Strong.

17

I am doubtful whether I was at heart glad or sorry when my school days drew to an end, and the time came for my leaving Doctor Strong's. I had been very happy there, I had a great attachment for the Doctor, but misty ideas of being a young man at my own disposal lured me away.

My aunt and I had held many grave deliberations on the calling to which I should be devoted. For a year or more I had endeavoured to find a satisfactory answer to her often-repeated question, 'What I would like to be?' But I had no particular liking, that I could discover, for anything.

'Trot, I tell you what, my dear,' said my aunt, one morning in the Christmas season when I left school: 'as this knotty point is still unsettled, and as we must not make a mistake in our decision if we can help it, I think we had better take a little breathing-time. Suppose you were to go down into the old part of the country again, for instance, and see that – that out-of-the-way woman with the savagest of names,' said my aunt, rubbing her nose, for she could never thoroughly forgive Peggotty for being so called.

'Of all things in the world, aunt, I should like it best!'

'But you may begin, in a small way, to have a reliance upon yourself, and to act for yourself,' said my aunt. 'I shall send you upon your trip, alone. I did think, once, of Mr Dick's going with you; but, on second thoughts, I shall keep him to take care of me.'

Mr Dick, for a moment, looked a little disappointed; until the honour and dignity of having to take care of the most wonderful woman in the world, restored the sunshine to his face.

'Besides,' said my aunt, 'there's the Memorial.'

'Oh, certainly,' said Mr Dick, in a hurry, 'I intend, Trotwood, to get that done immediately – it really must be done immediately!'

In pursuance of my aunt's kind scheme, I was shortly afterwards fitted out with a handsome purse of money, and portmanteau, and tenderly dismissed upon my expedition. At parting, my aunt gave me some good advice, and a good many kisses; and said that as her object was that I would look about me, and should think a little, she would recommend me to stay a few days in London, if I liked it, either on my way down to Suffolk, or in coming back.

I went to Canterbury first, that I might take leave of Agnes and Mr Wickfield (my old room in whose house I had not yet relinquished). Agnes was very glad to see me, and told me that the house had not been like itself since I left it.

'I am sure I am not like myself when I am away,' I said. 'I seem to want my right hand, when I miss you. Everyone who knows you consults with you, and is guided by you, Agnes.'

'Everyone who knows me spoils me, I believe,' she said, smiling.

'No. It's because you are like no one else. You are so good, and so sweet-tempered. You have such a gentle nature, and you are always right.'

Agnes laughed again, and shook her head. Now suddenly lifting up her eyes to mine, she said:

'Trotwood, there is something that I want to ask you, and that I may not have another opportunity of asking for a long time, perhaps. Have you observed any gradual alteration in papa?'

I had observed it, and had often wondered whether she had too. I must have shown as much, now, in my face; for her eyes were in a moment cast down, and I saw tears in them.

'Tell me what it is,' she said.

'Shall I be quite plain, Agnes, liking him so much?'

'Yes,' she said.

'His hand trembles, his speech is not plain, and his eyes look wild at those times when he is most certain to be wanted on some business.'

'By Uriah?' said Agnes.

'Yes,' I said.

*

Morning brought with it my parting from the old house, which Agnes had filled with her influence. I was heavier at heart, when I packed up such of my books and clothes as still remained there to be sent to Dover, than I cared to show to Uriah Heep; who was so officious to help me that I uncharitably thought him mighty glad that I was going.

I got away from Agnes and her father, somehow, with an indifferent show of being very manly, and took my seat upon the box of the London coach.

We went to the Golden Cross at Charing Cross, then a mouldy sort of establishment in a close neighbourhood. A waiter showed me into the coffee-room; and a chambermaid introduced me to my small bedchamber, which smelt like a hackney-coach, and was shut up like a family vault. I was still painfully conscious of my youth, for nobody stood in any awe of me at all: the chambermaid being utterly indifferent to my opinions on any subject, and the waiter being familiar with me, and offering advice to my inexperience.

Being in a pleasant frame of mind after dinner, I resolved to go to the play. It was Covent Garden Theatre that I chose; and there, from the back of the centre box, I saw *Julius Caesar* and the new Pantomime. To have all those noble Romans alive before me, and walking in and out for my entertainment, instead of being the stern taskmasters they had been at school, was a most novel and delightful effect.

But the mingled reality and mystery of the whole show, the influence upon me of the poetry, the lights, the music, the company, the smooth stupendous changes of flittering and brilliant scenery, were so dazzling, that when I came out into the rainy street, at twelve o'clock at night, I felt as if I had come from the clouds.

I stood in the street for a little while, as if I really were a stranger upon earth: but the unceremonious pushing and hustling that I received soon recalled me to myself, and put me in the road back to the hotel. Thither I went, revolving the glorious vision all the way: and there, after some porter and oysters, I sat revolving it still, at past one o'clock, with my eyes on the coffee-room fire.

I was so filled with the play and with the past, that I don't know when the figure of a handsome well-formed young man, dressed with a tasteful easy negligence, became a real presence to me. But I went up to him at once.

'Steerforth! won't you speak to me?'

He looked at me.

'My God! It's little Copperfield!'

I grasped him by both hands, and could not let them go.

'I never, never, never was so glad! My dear Steerforth, I am so overjoyed to see you!'

'And I am rejoiced to see you, too!' he said, shaking my hands heartily, and we sat down together, side by side.

'Why, how do you come to be here?' said Steerforth, clapping me on the shoulder.

'I came here by the Canterbury coach, today. I have been adopted by an aunt down in that part of the country, and have just finished my education there. How do *you* come to be here, Steerforth?'

'Well, I am what they call "an Oxford man", and I am on my way now to my mother's. I remained here tonight instead of going on. I have been dozing and grumbling away at the play.'

'I have been at the play, too,' said I. 'At Covent Garden. What a delightful and magnificent entertainment, Steerforth!'

Steerforth laughed heartily.

'My dear young Davy,' he said, clapping me on the shoulder again, 'you are a very Daisy. The daisy of the field, at sunrise, is not fresher than you are. I have been at Covent Garden, too, and there never was a more miserable business. Holloa, you sir!'

This was addressed to the waiter, who had been very attentive to our recognition, at a distance, and now came forward deferentially.

'Where have you put my friend, Mr Copperfield?' said Steerforth.

'Well, sir,' said the waiter, with an apologetic air. 'Mr Copperfield is at present in forty-four, sir.'

'And what the devil do you mean,' retorted Steerforth, 'by putting Mr Copperfield into a little loft over a stable?'

'Why, you see we wasn't aware, sir, as Mr Copperfield was anyways particular. We can give Mr Copperfield seventy-two, sir, if it would be preferred. Next to you, sir.'

'Of course it would be preferred,' said Steerforth. 'And do it at once.'

I found my new room a great improvement on my old one, it having an immense four-post bedstead in it, which was quite a little landed estate. Here, among pillows enough for six, I soon fell asleep.

18

Next morning I found Steerforth in a snug private apartment, red-curtained and Turkey-carpeted, where the fire burnt bright, and a fine hot breakfast was set forth on a table covered with a clean cloth.

'Now, Copperfield,' he said, 'I should like to hear what you are doing, and where you are going, and all about you.'

I told him how my aunt had proposed the little expedition that I had before me, and whither it tended.

'As you are in no hurry, then,' said Steerforth, 'come home with me to Highgate, and stay a day or two. You will be pleased with my mother, and she will be pleased with you.'

After I had written to my aunt and told her of my fortunate meeting with my admired old schoolfellow, and my acceptance of his invitation, we went out in a hackney-chariot, and saw a Panorama and some other sights, and took a walk through the Museum.

Lunch succeeded to our sight-seeing, and the short winter day wore away so fast, that it was dusk when the stage-coach stopped with us at an old brick house at High-gate on the summit of the hill. An elderly lady, though not very far advanced in years, with a proud carriage and a handsome face, was in the doorway as we alighted; and greeting Steerforth as 'My dearest James,' folded him in her arms. This lady he presented to me as his mother, and she gave me a stately welcome.

It was a genteel old-fashioned house, very quiet and orderly. I had little time to dress before I was called to dinner.

There was a second lady in the dining-room, of a slight short figure, who attracted my attention. She had black hair and eager black eyes, and was thin, and had a scar upon her lip. It was an old scar – I should rather call it seam, for it was not discoloured, and had healed years ago – which had once cut through her mouth, downward towards the chin, but was now barely visible across the table. Her thinness seemed to be the effect of some wasting fire within her, which found a vent in her gaunt eyes.

She was introduced as Miss Dartle, and both Steerforth and his mother called her Rosa. I found that she lived there, and had been for a long time Mrs Steerforth's companion. It appeared to me that she never said outright anything she wanted to say, but hinted it, and made a great deal more of it by this practice.

For example, when Mrs Steerforth observed, more in jest than earnest, that she feared her son led but a wild life at college, Miss Dartle put in:

'Oh, really? You know how ignorant I am, and that I only ask for information, but isn't it always so? I thought that kind of life was on all hands understood to be – eh?'

'My son's tutor is a conscientious gentleman,' said Mrs Steerforth, 'and if I had not implicit reliance upon my son, I should have reliance on him.'

'Should you?' said Miss Dartle. 'How very nice! What a comfort! Really conscientious? Then he's not ... but of course he can't be, if he's really conscientious. Well, I shall be quite happy in my opinion of him, from this time. You can't think how it elevates him in my opinion, to know for certain that he's really conscientious!'

When she was gone, and Steerforth and I were sitting before the fire, he asked me what I thought of her.

'She is very clever, is she not?' I said.

'Clever! She brings everything to a grindstone,' said Steerforth, 'and sharpens it, as she has sharpened her own face and figure these past years. She has worn herself away by constant sharpening. She is all edge.'

'What a remarkable scar that is upon her lip!' I said.

Steerforth's face fell, and he paused a moment.

'Why, the fact is, I did that.'

'By an unfortunate accident?'

'No. I was a young boy, and she exasperated me, and I threw a hammer at her. A promising young angel I must have been!'

I was deeply sorry to have touched on such a painful theme, but that was useless now.

'She has borne the mark ever since, as you see,' said Steerforth; 'and she'll bear it to her grave.'

I could not help glancing at the scar with a painful interest when we went in to tea. It was not long before I observed that it was the most susceptible part of her face. There was a little altercation between her and Steerforth about a cast of the dice at back-gammon – when I thought her, for one moment, in a storm of rage; and then I saw it start forth like the old writing on the wall.

When the evening was pretty far spent, and a tray of glasses and decanters came in, Steerforth promised, over the fire, that he would seriously think of going down into the country with me. While we were talking, he more than once called me Daisy; which brought Miss Dartle out again.

'But really, Mr Copperfield,' she asked, 'is it a nick-name? And why does he give it to you? Is it – eh – because he thinks you young and innocent? I am so stupid in these things.'

I coloured in replying that I believed it was.

'Oh!' said Miss Dartle. 'Now I am glad to know that! I ask for information, and I am glad to know it. He thinks you young and innocent; and so you are his friend. Well, that's quite delightful!'

She went to bed soon after this, and Mrs Steerforth retired too. Steerforth and I lingered for half-an-hour over the fire, talking about Traddles and all the rest of them at old Salem House.

19

There was a servant in that house, a man who, I understood, was usually with Steerforth and had come into
his service at the University, who was in appearance a
pattern of respectability. I believe there never existed in his
station a more respectable-looking man. He was taciturn,
soft-footed, very quiet in his manner, deferential, observant,
always at hand when wanted, and never near when not
wanted. It would have been next to impossible to suspect
him of anything wrong, he was so thoroughly respectable.

Such a self-contained man I never saw. Even the fact that
no one knew his Christian name, seemed to form a part of
his respectability. Nothing could be objected against his
surname, Littimer, by which he was known. Peter might
have been hanged, or Tom transported: but Littimer was
perfectly respectable.

Littimer got horses for us; and Steerforth, who knew
everything, gave me lessons in riding. He provided foils for
us, and Steerforth gave me lessons in fencing – gloves, and
I began, of the same master, to improve in boxing. It gave

me no manner of concern that Steerforth should find me a novice in these sciences, but I never could bear to show my want of skill before the respectable Littimer.

I am particular about this man, because he made a particular effect on me at that time, and because of what took place thereafter.

A week passed away in a most delightful manner, and the day arrived for our departure. We bade adieu to Mrs Steerforth and Miss Dartle, with many thanks on my part. The last thing I saw was Littimer's unruffled eye; fraught, as I fancied, with the silent conviction that I was very young indeed.

What I felt, in returning so auspiciously to the old familiar places, I shall not endeavour to describe. We drove through Yarmouth's dark streets to the inn, went to bed on our arrival, and breakfasted late in the morning. Steerforth, who was in great spirits, had been strolling about the beach before I was up, and had made acquaintance, he said, with half the boatmen in the place. Moreover, he had seen, in the distance, what he was sure must be the identical house of Mr Peggotty, with smoke coming out of the chimney.

'When do you propose to introduce me there, Daisy?' he said. 'I am at your disposal. Make your own arrangements.'

'Why, I was thinking that this evening would be a good time, Steerforth, when they are all sitting round the fire. I should like you to see it when it's snug, it's such a curious place.'

'So be it!' returned Steerforth. 'This evening.'

Meanwhile I went away to my dear old Peggotty's.

Here she was, in the tiled kitchen, cooking dinner! The moment I knocked at the door she opened it, and asked me what I pleased to want. I looked at her with a smile, but she gave me no smile in return. I had never ceased to write to her, but it must have been seven years since we had met.

'Is Mr Barkis at home, ma'am?' I said.

'He's at home, sir, but he's abed with rheumatics.'

'Don't he go over to Blunderstone now?' I asked.

She took a step backward, and put out her hands in an undecided frightened way.

'Peggotty!' I cried to her.

She cried, 'My darling boy!' and we both burst into tears, and were locked in one another's arms. I had never laughed and cried in all my life, more freely than I did that morning.

'Barkis will be so glad,' said Peggotty, wiping her eyes with her apron, 'that it'll do him more good than pints of liniment. May I go and tell him you are here? Will you come up and see him, my dear?'

Of course I would.

Mr Barkis received me with absolute enthusiasm. He was too rheumatic to be shaken hands with, but he begged me to shake the tassel on the top of his nightcap, which I did most cordially. When I sat down by the side of the bed, he said that it did him a world of good to feel as if he was driving me on the Blunderstone road again.

I prepared Peggotty for Steerforth's arrival, and it was not long before he came. His easy, spirited good humour, his genial manner, his handsome looks, his natural gift of adapting himself to whomsoever he pleased, and making direct, when he cared to do it, to the main point of interest in anybody's heart, bound her to him wholly in five minutes. His manner to me, alone, would have won her. But, through all these causes combined, I sincerely believe she had a kind of adoration for him before he left the house that night.

He stayed there with me to dinner – if I were to say willingly, I should not half express how readily and gaily. He went into Mr Barkis's room like light and air, brightening and refreshing it as if he were healthy weather.

He maintained all his delightful qualities to the last, until we started forth, at eight o'clock, for Mr Peggotty's boat.

As we approached, a murmur of voices had been audible and, at the moment of our entrance, a clapping of hands: which latter noise, I was surprised to see, proceeded from the generally disconsolate Mrs Gummidge.

But Mrs Gummidge was not the only person there who was unusually excited. Mr Peggotty, his face lighted up with uncommon satisfaction, and laughing with all his might, held his rough arms wide open, as if for little Em'ly to run into them; Ham, with a mixed expression on his face of admiration, exultation, and a lumbering sort of bashfulness that sat upon him very well, held little Em'ly by the hand, as if he were presenting her to Mr Peggotty.

Little Em'ly herself, blushing and shy, but delighted with Mr Peggotty's delight, as her joyous eyes expressed, was stopped by our entrance (for she saw us first) in the very act of springing from Ham to nestle in Mr Peggotty's embrace.

The little picture was so instantaneously dissolved by our going in, that one might have doubted whether it had ever been. I was in the midst of the astonished family, face to face with Mr Peggotty, and holding out my hand to him, when Ham shouted:

'Mas'r Davy! It's Mas'r Davy!'

In a moment we were all shaking hands with one another, and asking one another how we did, and telling one another how glad we were to meet, and all talking at once. Mr Peggotty was so proud and overjoyed to see us, that he did not know what to say or do, but kept over and over again shaking hands with me, and then with Steerforth.

I thought I had never seen Ham grin to anything like the extent to which he sat grinning at us now.

'What does this here blessed tarpaulin go and do,' said Mr Peggotty, with his face one high noon of enjoyment, 'but he loses that there art of his to our little Em'ly. All of a sudden, one evening – as if it might be tonight – comes little Em'ly from her work, and him with her! And he cries out to me, joyful, "Look here! This is to be my little wife!"'

And she says, half bold and half shy, and half a laughing and half a crying, "Yes, Uncle! If you please." – If I please!' cried Mr Peggotty, rolling his head in an ecstasy at the idea; 'Lord, as if I should do anythink else.'

20

Steerforth and I stayed for more than a fortnight in that part of the country. We were very much together, I need not say; but occasionally we were asunder for some hours at a time. He was a good sailor, and I was but an indifferent one; and when he went out boating with Mr Peggotty, which was a favourite amusement of his, I generally remained ashore.

One dark evening, when I was later than usual – for I had, that day, been making my parting visit to Blunderstone, as we were now about to return home – I found him alone in Mr Peggotty's house, sitting thoughtfully before the fire.

'I've taken a fancy to the place,' he said. 'At all events, I have bought a boat that was for sale – a clipper, Mr Peggotty says; and so she is – and Mr Peggotty will be master of her in my absence.'

'I understand you, Steerforth!' I said. 'You pretend to have bought it for yourself, but you have really done so to confer a benefit on him. I might have known as much at first, knowing you. My dear kind Steerforth, how can I tell you what I think of your generosity?'

'Tush!' he answered, turning red. 'Anyway, she must be newly rigged and I shall leave Littimer behind to see it done, that I may know she is quite complete. Did I tell you Littimer had come down?'

'No.'

'Oh, yes! came down this morning, with a letter from my mother. He shall see to the boat being fresh named. She's the Stormy Petrel now. What does Mr Peggotty care for Stormy Petrels! I'll have her christened again.'

'By what name?' I asked.

'The Little Em'ly.'

21

Next morning, while we were at breakfast, a letter was delivered to me from my aunt. As it contained matter on which I thought Steerforth could advise me as well as anyone, I resolved to make it a subject of discussion on our journey home.

For the present we had enough to do, in taking leave of all our friends. Mr Barkis was far from being the last among them in his regret at our departure. Peggotty and all her family were full of grief at our going; and there were so many seafaring volunteers in attendance on Steerforth, when our portmanteaux went to the coach, that if we had had the baggage of a regiment with us, we should hardly have wanted porters to carry it. In a word, we departed to the regret and admiration of all concerned, and left a great many people very sorry behind us.

'Do you stay long here, Littimer?' I said, as he stood waiting to see the coach start.

'No, sir,' he replied. 'Probably not very long, sir.'

'He can hardly say, just now,' observed Steerforth carelessly. 'He knows what he has to do, and he'll do it.'

We left him standing on the pavement, as respectable a mystery as any pyramid in Egypt.

For some little time we held no conversation. At length Steerforth, becoming gay and talkative in a moment, pulled me by the arm.

'Find a voice, David. What about that letter you were speaking of at breakfast?'

'Oh!' I said, taking it out of my pocket. 'It's from my aunt. She asks me, here, if I think I should like to be a proctor. What do you think of it?'

'Well, I don't know,' replied Steerforth. 'You may as well do that as anything else, I suppose.'

I could not help laughing at his balancing all callings and professions so equally.

'What *is* a proctor, Steerforth?'

'Why, he is a sort of monkish attorney to some faded courts held in the Doctors' Commons – a lazy old nook near St Paul's Churchyard. Doctors' Commons is a little out-of- the-way place that has an ancient monopoly in suits about people's wills and people's marriages, and disputes among ships and boats.'

'Nonsense, Steerforth!' I said. 'You don't mean to say that there is any affinity between nautical matters and ecclesiastical matters?'

'I don't, indeed, my dear boy. But I mean to say that they

are managed and decided by the same set of people, down in that same Doctors' Commons.'

I made allowance for Steerforth's light way of treating the subject, and did not feel indisposed towards my aunt's suggestion, which she left to my free decision, making no scruple of telling me that it had occurred to her on her lately visiting her own proctor in Doctors' Commons for the purpose of settling her will in my favour.

'That's a laudable proceeding on the part of your aunt, at all events,' said Steerforth, when I mentioned it; 'and one deserving of all encouragements. Daisy, my advice is that you take kindly to Doctors' Commons.'

I quite made up my mind to do so. I then told Steerforth that my aunt was in town awaiting me (as I found from her letter), and that she had taken lodgings for a week at a kind of private hotel in Lincoln's Inn Fields.

When we came to our journey's end, he went home, engaging to call upon me the next day but one; and I drove to Lincoln's Inn Fields, where I found my aunt up, and awaiting supper.

If I had been round the world since we parted, we could hardly have been better pleased to meet again. My aunt cried outright as she embraced me.

Supper was comfortably served and hot, and when the table was cleared, Janet assisted my aunt to arrange her hair, and to put on her nightcap, which was of a smarter construction than usual ('in case of fire', my aunt said). I then made her, according to certain established regulations from which no deviation, however slight, could ever be permitted, a glass of hot wine and water, and a slice of toast cut into long thin strips.

With these accompaniments we were left alone to finish the evening, my aunt sitting opposite me drinking her wine and water, soaking her strips of toast in it, one by one, before eating them; and looking benignly on me from among the borders of her nightcap.

'Well, Trot,' she began, 'what do you think of the proctor plan? Or have you not begun to think about it yet?'

'I have thought a good deal about it, my dear aunt, and I have talked a good deal about it with Steerforth. I like it very much indeed. I like it exceedingly.'

'Come!' said my aunt. 'That's cheering.'

'I have only one difficulty, aunt.'

'Say what it is, Trot.'

'Why, I want to ask, aunt, as this seems to be a limited profession, whether my entrance into it would not be very expensive?'

'It will cost,' returned my aunt, 'to article you, just a thousand pounds.'

'Now, my dear aunt,' I said, drawing my chair nearer, 'I am uneasy in my mind about that. It's a large sum of money. You have expended a great deal on my education, and have always been the soul of generosity. Surely there are some ways in which I might begin life with hardly any outlay, and yet with a good hope of getting on by resolution and exertion. Are you sure that it would not be better to try that course?'

My aunt finished eating the piece of toast on which she was then engaged and looked me full in the face.

'Trot, my child, if I have any object in life, it is to provide for your being a good, a sensible, and a happy man. I am bent upon it – so is Dick. From the time you came to me, a little runaway boy, all dusty and way-worn, you have ever been a credit to me and a pride and a pleasure. I have no other claim upon my means; at least' – here to my surprise she hesitated, and was confused – 'no, I have *no* other claim upon my means – and you are my adopted child. Only be a loving child to me in my age, and bear with my whims and fancies; and you will do more for an old woman whose prime of life was not so happy or conciliating as it might have been, than ever that old woman did for you.'

The following morning we set out for the office of Messrs Spenlow and Jorkins, in Doctors' Commons. My aunt, who had the general opinion that every man she saw in London was a pickpocket, gave me her purse to carry for her, which had ten guineas in it and some silver.

We made a pause at the toy-shop in Fleet Street, to see the giants of St Dunstan's strike upon the bells – we had timed our going, so as to catch them at it, at twelve o'clock – and then went on towards Ludgate Hill, and St Paul's Churchyard. We were crossing to the former place, when I found that my aunt greatly accelerated her speed, and looked frightened. I observed, at the same time, that a lowering, ill-dressed man was coming so close after us as to brush against her.

'Trot! My dear Trot!' cried my aunt, pressing my arm. 'I don't know what I am to do.'

'Don't be alarmed,' I said. 'There's nothing to be afraid of. Step into a shop, and I'll soon get rid of this fellow.'

We had stopped in an empty doorway, while this was passing, and he had stopped too.

'Don't look at him!' said my aunt, as I turned my head indignantly, 'but get me a coach, my dear, and wait for me in St Paul's Churchyard.'

'Wait for you?'

'Yes,' said my aunt. 'I must go alone. I must go with him.'

'With him, aunt? This man?'

'I am in my senses,' she replied, 'and I tell you I *must*. Get me a coach!'

However much astonished I might be, I had no right to refuse compliance. I hurried away a few paces, and called a hackney-chariot which was passing empty. Almost before I could let down the steps, my aunt sprang in, I don't know how, and the man followed. She waved her hand to me to go away, so earnestly that, all confounded as I was, I turned from them at once. In doing so, I heard her say to the coachman, 'Drive anywhere! Drive straight on!' and presently the chariot passed me, going up the hill.

After half-an-hour's cooling in the churchyard, I saw the chariot coming back. The driver stopped beside me, and my aunt was sitting in it alone. She said no more, except: 'My dear child, never ask me what it was, and don't refer to it,' until she had perfectly regained her composure, when she told me she was quite herself now and we might get out. On her giving me her purse to pay the driver, I found that all the guineas were gone, and only the loose silver remained.

Doctors' Commons was approached by a little low archway. Before we had taken many paces down the street beyond it, the noise of the city seemed to melt, as if by magic, into a softened distance. A few dull courts and narrow ways brought us to the sky-lighted offices of Spenlow and Jorkins.

Mr Spenlow was a little light-haired gentleman, with the stiffest of white cravats and shirt-collars. He was got up with such care, and was so stiff, that he could hardly bend himself, being obliged, when he glanced at some papers on his desk, to move his whole body, from the bottom of his spine, like Punch.

I had previously been presented by my aunt, and had been courteously received. He now said:

'And so, Mr Copperfield, you think of entering into our profession? I casually mentioned to Miss Trotwood, when I had the pleasure of an interview with her the other day,' – an inclination of his body: Punch again – 'that there was a vacancy here. Miss Trotwood was good enough to mention that she had a nephew who was her peculiar care, and for whom she was seeking to provide genteelly in life. That nephew, I believe, I now have the pleasure of' – Punch again.

I bowed my acknowledgements, and said that my aunt had mentioned to me that there was that opening, and that I believed I should like it very much, but that I presumed I should have an opportunity of trying how I liked it, before I bound myself to it irrevocably.

'Oh, surely! surely!' said Mr Spenlow. 'We always, in this house, propose an initiatory month. I should be happy, myself, to propose two months – three – an indefinite period, in fact – but I have a partner. Mr Jorkins.'

'And the premium, sir,' I said, 'is a thousand pounds?'

'And the premium, Stamp included, is a thousand pounds. As I have mentioned to Miss Trotwood, I am actu-ated by no mercenary considerations – few men less so, I believe – but Mr Jorkins has opinions on these subjects, and I am bound to respect Mr Jorkins's opinions. Mr Jorkins thinks a thousand pounds too little, in short.'

'I suppose, sir,' I said, still desiring to spare my aunt, 'that it is not the custom here, if an articled clerk were particu-larly useful, to allow him . . .'

Anticipating the word 'salary', Mr Spenlow, by a great effort, just lifted his head far enough out of his cravat to shake it.

'No. I will not say what consideration I might give to that point myself, Mr Copperfield, if I were unfettered. Mr Jorkins is immovable.'

I was quite dismayed by the idea of this terrible Jorkins. But I found out afterwards that he was a mild man, whose place in the business was to keep himself in the background and be constantly exhibited by name as the most obdurate and ruthless of men. If a clerk wanted his salary raised, Mr Jorkins wouldn't listen to such a proposition. If a client were slow to settle his bill of costs, Mr Jorkins was resolved to have it paid – and however painful these things might be (and always were) to the feelings of Mr Spenlow, Mr Jorkins would have his bond. The heart and the hand of the good angel Spenlow would always have been open, but for the restraining demon Jorkins.

It was settled that I should begin my month's probation as soon as I pleased.

We arrived at Lincoln's Inn Fields without any new adventures. I knew my aunt was anxious to get home and I now urged her to leave me to take care of myself.

'I have not been here a week to-morrow, without considering that too, my dear,' she returned. 'There is a furnished little set of chambers to be let in the Adelphi, Trot, which ought to suit you to a marvel.'

She produced from her pocket an advertisement, carefully cut out of a newspaper, setting forth that in Buckingham Street in the Adelphi there was to be let, furnished, with a view of the river, a singularly desirable, and compact set of chambers, with immediate possession. Terms moderate.

'Why, this is the very thing, aunt!' I said, flushed with the possible dignity of living in chambers.

'Then come,' replied my aunt, immediately resuming the bonnet she had a minute before laid aside. 'We'll go and look at 'em.'

Away we went. The advertisement directed us to apply to Mrs Crupp on the premises.

Mrs Crupp was a stout lady with a flounce of flannel petticoat below a nankeen gown.

'Let us see these chambers of yours, if you please, ma'am,' said my aunt.

They were on the top of the house – a great point with my aunt, being near the fire-escape – and consisted of a little half-blind entry where you could hardly see anything, a little stone-blind pantry where you could see nothing at all, a sitting-room, and a bedroom. The furniture was rather faded, but quite good enough for me; and, sure enough, the river was outside the windows.

As I was delighted with the place, my aunt and Mrs Crupp withdrew into the pantry to discuss the terms, while I remained on the sitting-room sofa, hardly daring to think it possible that I could be destined to live in such a noble residence.

After a single combat of some duration they returned,

and I saw, to my joy, both in Mrs Crupp's countenance and in my aunt's, that the deed was done.

In short, my aunt, seeing how enraptured I was with the premises, took them for a month, with leave to remain for twelve months when the time was out. Mrs Crupp was to find linen, and to cook; every other necessary was already provided; and Mrs Crupp expressly intimated that she should always yearn towards me as a son.

22

It was a wonderfully fine thing to have that lofty castle to myself, and to feel, when I shut my outer door, like Robinson Crusoe when he had got into his fortification and pulled his ladder up after him. It was a wonderfully fine thing to walk about town with the key of my house in my pocket.

After two days and nights, I felt as if I had lived there for a year.

Steerforth not yet appearing, which induced me to apprehend that he must be ill, I left Commons early on the third day, and walked out to Highgate.

Mrs Steerforth was very glad to see me, and said that he had gone away with one of his Oxford friends to see another who lived near St Albans, but that she expected him to return to-morrow.

As she pressed me to stay to dinner, I remained, and believe we talked about nothing but him all day. I told her how much the people liked him at Yarmouth, and what a delightful companion he had been. Miss Dartle was full of hints and mysterious questions, but took a great interest in all our proceedings there, and said, 'Was it really, though?' and so forth, so often, that she got everything out of me she wanted to know.

I was taking my coffee and roll in the morning, before going to the Commons, when Steerforth himself walked in, to my unbounded joy.

I showed him over the establishment, with no little pride, and he commended it highly.

'I tell you what, old boy,' he said, 'I shall make quite a town house of this, unless you give me notice to quit.'

This was a delightful hearing.

'Then you'll come to dinner?' I said.

'I can't, upon my life. There's nothing I should like better, but I *must* remain with these two fellows. We are all three off together to-morrow morning.'

'Then bring them here to dinner,' I returned.

When he was gone, I rang for Mrs Crupp, and acquainted her with my desperate design.

Walking along the Strand afterwards, I gave a rather extensive order at a retail wine-merchant's.

When I came home in the afternoon, and saw the bottles drawn up in a square on the pantry floor, they looked so numerous (though there were two missing, which made Mrs Crupp very uncomfortable), that I was absolutely frightened at them.

One of Steerforth's friends was named Grainger, and

the other Markham. They were both very lively fellows.

Being a little embarrassed at first, and feeling much too young to preside, I made Steerforth take the head of the table when dinner was announced, and seated myself opposite to him.

Everything was very good; we did not spare the wine; and he exerted himself so brilliantly to make things pass off well, that there was no pause in our festivity. I abandoned myself to enjoyment.

I laughed heartily at my own jokes, and everybody else's; called Steerforth to order for not passing the wine; made several engagements to go to Oxford: and announced that I meant to have a dinner-party exactly like that, once a week, until further notice.

I went on by passing the wine faster and faster yet, and continually starting up with a corkscrew to open more wine, long before any was needed.

Somebody was smoking. We were all smoking. *I* was smoking, and trying to suppress a rising tendency to shudder.

Somebody was leaning out of my bedroom window, refreshing his forehead against the cool stone of the parapet, and feeling the air upon his face. It was myself. Now, somebody was unsteadily contemplating his features in the looking-glass. That was I too. I was very pale in the looking-glass; my eyes had a vacant appearance; and my hair – only my hair, nothing else – looked drunk.

Somebody said to me: 'Let us go to the theatre, Copperfield!'

We went downstairs, one behind another. Near the bottom, somebody fell, and rolled down. Somebody else said it was Copperfield. I was angry at that false report, until, finding myself on my back in the passage, I began to think there might be some foundation for it.

A very foggy night, with great rings round the lamps in the streets!

Shortly afterwards, we were very high up in a very hot theatre, looking down into a large pit, that seemed to me to smoke. There was a great stage, too, and there were people upon it, talking about something or other, but not at all intelligibly. There was an abundance of bright lights, and there was music, and there were ladies down in the boxes, and I don't know what more. The whole building looked to me as if it were learning to swim.

On somebody's motion, we resolved to go downstairs to the dress-boxes, where the ladies were.

I was being ushered into one of these boxes, and found myself saying something as I sat down, and people about me crying 'Silence!' to somebody, and – what! yes! – Agnes, sitting on the seat before me, in the same box, with a lady and gentleman beside her, whom I didn't know. I see her face now, better than I did then, I dare say, with its indelible look of regret and wonder turned upon me.

'Agnes!' I said, thickly. 'Lorblessmer! Agnes!'

'Hush! pray!' she answered. I could not conceive why.

'I know you will do as I ask you, if I tell you I am very earnest in it. Go away now, Trotwood, for my sake, and ask your friends to take you home.'

She had so far improved me, for the time, that though I was angry with her, I felt ashamed, and with a short 'Goori!' (which I intended for 'Goodnight!') got up and went away.

I stepped at once out of the box-door into my bedroom, where Steerforth was with me, helping me to undress.

The agony of mind, the remorse, and shame I felt when I became conscious next day! My recollection of that indelible look which Agnes had given me – my racking head – the smell of smoke, the sight of glasses, the impossibility of going out, or even getting up! Oh, what a day it was!

23

The next morning I was going out at my door when I saw a ticket-porter coming upstairs, with a letter in his hand.

'T. Copperfield, Esquire,' said the ticket-porter, touching his hat with his little cane, and gave me the letter, which he said required an answer. I shut him out on the landing to wait for the answer, and went into my chambers again.

I found that it was a very kind note, containing no reference to my condition at the theatre. All it said was:

'My dear Trotwood. I am staying at the house of papa's agent, Mr Waterbrook, in Ely Place, Holborn. Will you come and see me today, at any time you like to appoint? Ever yours affectionately, Agnes.'

It took me such a long time to write an answer at all to my satisfaction, that I don't know what the ticket-porter can have thought. After many attempts, I wrote:

'My dear Agnes. Your letter is like you, and what could I say of it that would be higher praise than that? I will come at four o'clock. Affectionately and sorrowfully, T.C.'

The professional business of Mr Waterbrook's establishment was done on the ground-floor, and the genteel business (of which there was a good deal) in the upper part of the building. I was shown into a pretty but rather close drawing-room, and there sat Agnes.

She looked so quiet and good, and reminded me so strongly of my airy fresh school days at Canterbury, and the sodden, smoky, stupid wretch I had been the other night, that, nobody being by, I yielded to my self-reproach and shame, and – in short, made a fool of myself.

'If it had been anyone but you, Agnes,' I said, turning away my head, 'I should not have minded it half so much. But that it should have been you who saw me! I almost wish I had been dead, first.'

She put her hand – its touch was like no other hand – upon my arm for a moment; and I felt so befriended and comforted, that I could not help moving it to my lips, and gratefully kissing it.

'You are my good Angel!'

'If I were, indeed, Trotwood,' she returned, 'there is one thing that I should set my heart on very much.'

I looked at her inquiringly.

'On warning you,' said Agnes, with a steady glance, 'against your bad Angel.'

'My dear Agnes,' I began, 'if you mean Steerforth –'

'I do, Trotwood.'

'Then, Agnes, you wrong him very much. Now, is it not

unjust, and unlike you, to judge him from what you saw of me the other night?'

'I do not judge him from what I saw of you the other night,' she said. 'I judge him, partly from your account of him, Trotwood, and your character, and the influence he has over you. You have made a dangerous friend.'

I looked at her, and his image, though it was still fixed in my heart, darkened.

'And when, Agnes,' I said, 'will you forgive me the other night?'

'When I recall it,' said Agnes.

Then she asked me if I had seen Uriah.

'Uriah Heep? No. Is he in London?'

'He comes to the office downstairs, every day,' said Agnes. 'He was in London a week before me. I am afraid on disagreeable business, Trotwood. I believe he is going to enter into partnership with papa.'

'What? Uriah? That mean, fawning fellow, worm himself into such promotion! You must prevent it, Agnes, while there's time.'

Agnes shook her head while I was speaking.

'You remember our last conversation about papa? It was not long after that – not more than two or three days – when he gave me the first intimation of what I tell you. Uriah has made himself indispensable to papa. He has mastered papa's weaknesses, fostered them, and taken advantage of them, until – until papa is afraid of him.'

Agnes had no time to say more, for the room door opened, and Mrs Waterbrook, who was a large lady – or who wore a large dress: I don't exactly know which, for I don't know which was dress and which was lady – came sailing in. I had a dim recollection of having seen her at the theatre, but she appeared to remember me perfectly and still to suspect me of being in a state of intoxication.

Finding by degrees, however, that I was sober, and (I hope) that I was a modest young gentleman, Mrs Waterbrook softened towards me considerably, and invited me to dinner next day.

When I arrived I found Uriah Heep among the company, in a suit of black, and in deep humility. He told me, when I shook hands with him, that he was proud to be noticed by me. I could have wished he had been less obliged to me, for he hovered about me in his gratitude all the rest of the evening; and whenever I said a word to Agnes, was sure, with his shadowless eyes and cadaverous face, to be looking gauntly down upon us from behind.

One guest attracted my attention before he came in, on account of my hearing him announced as Mr Traddles. My mind flew back to Salem House; could it be Tommy, I thought?

I made my way to Mr Waterbrook and said that I believed I had the pleasure of seeing an old schoolfellow there, and enquired what Mr Traddles was by profession.

'Traddles,' returned Mr Waterbrook, 'is a young man

reading for the bar. Yes. He is quite a good fellow – recommended to me by a professional friend. Oh yes. He has a kind of talent for stating a case in writing, plainly. I am able to throw something in Traddles's way, in the course of a year. Oh yes.'

Traddles and I were separated at table, being billeted in two remote corners. The dinner was very long, and the conversation was about the Aristocracy.

I was very glad indeed to get upstairs to Agnes, and to talk with her in a corner, and to introduce Traddles to her, who was shy, but agreeable. As he was obliged to leave early, on account of going away next morning for a month, I had not nearly so much conversation with him as I could have wished; but we exchanged addresses, and promised ourselves the pleasure of another meeting when he should come back to town.

24

I saw no more of Uriah Heep until the day when Agnes left town. I was at the coach office to take leave of her and see her go; and there was he, returning to Canterbury by the same conveyance.

At the coach window, as at the dinner-party, he hovered about us without a moment's intermission, like a great vulture gorging himself on every syllable that I said to Agnes, or Agnes said to me. A miserable foreboding oppressed me. Thus it was that we parted: she waving her hand and smiling farewell from the coach window; her evil genius writhing on the roof, as if he had her in his clutches and triumphed.

I had ample leisure to refine upon my uneasiness: for Steerforth was at Oxford, and when I was not at the Commons, I was very much alone.

In the meantime, days and weeks slipped away. I was articled to Spenlow and Jorkins. My rooms were engaged for twelve months certain.

On the day when I was articled, no festivity took place,

beyond my having sandwiches and sherry in the office for the clerks. Mr Spenlow remarked, on this occasion, that he should be happy to see me at his house at Norwood to celebrate our becoming connected.

Mr Spenlow was as good as his word. In a week or two, he referred to this engagement, and said that if I would do him the favour to come down next Saturday, and stay till Monday, he would be extremely happy.

When the day arrived, my very carpet-bag was an object of veneration to the stipendiary clerks, to whom the house at Norwood was a sacred mystery.

We were very pleasant, going down. Mr Spenlow gave me some hints in reference to my profession, and we talked about the Drama, and horses, until we came to Mr Spenlow's gate.

We went into the house, which was cheerfully lighted up, and turned into a room near at hand. I heard a voice say:

'Mr Copperfield, my daughter Dora, and my daughter Dora's confidential friend!'

It was, no doubt, Mr Spenlow's voice, but I didn't know it, and I didn't care whose it was. All was over in a moment. I had fulfilled my destiny. I was a captive and a slave. I loved Dora Spenlow to distraction!

'*I*,' observed a well-remembered voice, 'have seen Mr Copperfield before.'

The speaker was not Dora. No; the confidential friend – Miss Murdstone!

I don't think I was much astonished. To the best of my judgement, no capacity of astonishment was left in me. There was nothing worth mentioning in the material world, but Dora Spenlow, to be astonished about. I said:

'How do you do, Miss Murdstone? I hope you are well.'

She answered, 'Very well.'

I said, 'How is Mr Murdstone?'

She replied, 'My brother is robust, I am obliged to you.'

I have no idea what we had for dinner, besides Dora. My impression is, that I dined off Dora, entirely, and sent away half-a-dozen plates untouched. I sat next to her. I talked to her. She had the most delightful little voice, the gayest little laugh, the pleasantest and most fascinating little ways, that ever led a lost youth into hopeless slavery.

When she went out of the room with Miss Murdstone, I fell into a reverie, only disturbed by the cruel apprehension that Miss Murdstone would disparage me to her.

My apprehensions were revived when we went into the drawing-room, by the grim and distant aspect of Miss Murdstone. But I was relieved of them in an unexpected manner.

'David Copperfield,' said Miss Murdstone, beckoning me aside into a window. 'A word.'

I confronted Miss Murdstone alone.

'David Copperfield,' said Miss Murdstone, 'I need not enlarge upon family circumstances. They are not a tempting subject.'

'Far from it, ma'am,' I returned.

'Far from it,' assented Miss Murdstone. 'I shall not attempt to disguise the fact that I formed an unfavourable opinion of you in your childhood. It may have been a mistaken one, or you may have ceased to justify it. But it is not necessary that these opinions should come into collision here. Let us meet here as distant acquaintances. Do you approve of this?'

'Miss Murdstone,' I returned, 'I think you and Mr Murdstone used me very cruelly, and treated my mother with great unkindness. I shall always think so, as long as I live. But I quite agree in what you propose.'

All I know of the rest of the evening is that I heard the empress of my heart sing enchanted ballads in the French language, and I retired to bed in a most maudlin state of mind, and got up in a crisis of feeble infatuation.

How many cups of tea I drank, because Dora made it, I don't know. But I perfectly remember that I sat swilling tea until my whole nervous system, if I had had any in those days, must have gone by the board.

By and by we went to church. Miss Murdstone was between Dora and me in the pew; but I heard her sing, and the congregation vanished. A sermon was delivered – about Dora, of course – and I am afraid that is all I know of the service.

We had a quiet day. No company, a walk, a family dinner of four, and an evening of looking over books and pictures.

Ah! little did Mr Spenlow imagine, when I took leave of him at night, that he had just given his full consent to my being engaged to Dora, and that I was invoking blessings on his head!

25

The day after my return it came into my head to go and look up Traddles. He lived in a little street at Camden Town.

I found that the street was not as desirable a one as I could have wished it to be, for the sake of Traddles. The inhabitants appeared to have a propensity to throw any little trifles they were not in want of, into the road. I myself saw a shoe, a doubled-up saucepan, a black bonnet, and an umbrella, in various stages of decomposition, as I was looking out for the number I wanted.

The general air of the place reminded me forcibly of the days when I lived with Mr and Mrs Micawber.

'Traddles,' I said, shaking hands with him. 'I am delighted to see you.'

'I am delighted to see *you*, Copperfield,' he returned. 'I shan't conceal anything. You must know that I am engaged.'

Engaged! Oh, Dora!

'She is a curate's daughter,' said Traddles; 'one of ten, down in Devonshire. She is such a dear girl! We have made a beginning towards housekeeping. We must get on by degrees, but we have begun. Here,' drawing off the cloth with great pride and care, 'are two pieces of furniture to commence with. This flower-pot and stand, she bought herself.

'It's not a great deal towards the furnishing, but it's something. The table-cloths and pillow-cases, and articles of that kind, are what discourage me most, Copperfield. I don't make much, but I don't spend much. In general, I board with the people downstairs, who are very agreeable people indeed. Both Mr and Mrs Micawber have seen a good deal of life, and are excellent company.'

'Mr and Mrs Micawber!' I repeated. 'Why, I am intimately acquainted with them!'

An opportune double knock at the door, which I knew well from old experience in Windsor Terrace, and which nobody but Mr Micawber could ever have knocked at that door, resolved any doubt in my mind as to their being my old friends. I begged Traddles to ask his landlord to walk up. Traddles accordingly did so, over the banister; and Mr Micawber, not a bit changed – his tights, his stick, his shirt-collar, and his eye-glass, all the same as ever – came into the room with a genteel and youthful air.

'How do you do, Mr Micawber?' I said.

Mr Micawber fell back.

'Is it possible! Have I the pleasure of again beholding Copperfield!' and he shook me by both hands with the utmost fervour.

'You find us, Copperfield,' said Mr Micawber, with one eye on Traddles, 'at present established on what may be designated as a small and unassuming scale; but, you are aware that I have, in the course of my career, conquered obstacles. You find me fallen back – for a spring. I am at present, my dear Copperfield, engaged in the sale of corn, upon commission. It is not an avocation of a remunerative description – in other words, it does *not* pay – and some temporary embarrassments of a pecuniary nature have been the consequence. I am, however, delighted to add that I have now an immediate prospect of something turning up (I am not at liberty to say in what direction), which I trust will enable me to provide, permanently, both for myself and for your friend Traddles, in whom I have an unaffected interest.'

Mr Micawber then shook hands with me again, and left.

26

Next evening I was sitting by my fireside, when I heard a quick step ascending the stairs. As the step approached, I knew it, and felt my heart beat high, for it was Steerforth's.

I was never unmindful of Agnes, and she never left that sanctuary in my thoughts – if I may call it so – where I had placed her from the first. But when he entered, and stood before me with his hand out, the darkness that had fallen on him changed to light, and I felt confounded and ashamed of having doubted one I loved so heartily.

'Why, Daisy, old boy, dumb-foundered!' laughed Steerforth, shaking my hand heartily, and throwing it gaily away. 'Here's a supper for a king!' he exclaimed, taking his seat at the table. 'I shall do it justice, for I have come from Yarmouth.'

'I thought you came from Oxford?' I said.

'Not I,' said Steerforth. 'I have been seafaring – better employed.'

'Littimer was here today, to enquire for you,' I remarked, 'and I understood from him that you were at Oxford.'

'Littimer is a greater fool than I thought him, to have been enquiring for me at all,' said Steerforth, jovially pouring out a glass of wine, and drinking to me.

'So you have been at Yarmouth. Have you been there long?'

'No,' he said. 'An *escapade* of a week or so.'

'And how are they all? Of course, little Emily is not married yet?'

'Not yet. Going to be, I believe – in so many weeks, or months, or something or other. I have not seen much of 'em. By the by' – he laid down his knife and fork, which he had been using with great diligence, and began feeling in his pockets – 'I have a letter for you.'

'From whom?'

'Why, from your old nurse,' he said, taking some papers out of his breast pocket. 'Old what's-his-name's in a bad way, and it's about that, I believe.'

'Barkis, you mean?'

'Yes!' still feeling in his pockets, and looking over their contents: 'it's all over with poor Barkis, I am afraid.'

The letter was from Peggotty; something less legible than usual, and brief. It informed me of her husband's hopeless state.

'I tell you what, Steerforth. I think I will go down and see my old nurse. She is so attached to me that my visit will be a comfort and support to her.'

'You mean to go to-morrow, I suppose?' he said, holding me out at arm's length, with a hand on each of my shoulders.

'Yes, I think so.'

'Well, then, don't go till the next day. I wanted you to come and stay a few days with us. Here I am, on purpose to bid you, and you fly off to Yarmouth! Come! Say the next day!'

I said the next day.

27

Mrs Steerforth was pleased to see me, and so was Rosa Dartle. I was agreeably surprised to find that Littimer was not there, and that we were attended by a modest little parlour-maid, with blue ribbons in her cap.

Mrs Steerforth was particularly happy in her son's society, and Steerforth was, on this occasion, particularly attentive and respectful to her. It was very interesting to me to see them together, not only on account of their mutual affection, but because of the strong personal resemblance between them. I thought, more than once, that it was well no serious cause of division had ever come between them. The idea did not originate in my own discernment, I am bound to confess, but in a speech of Rosa Dartle's.

She said at dinner:

'Supposing – any unlikely thing will do for a supposition – that you and your mother were to have a serious quarrel.'

'My dear Rosa,' interposed Mrs Steerforth, laughing good-naturedly, 'suggest some other supposition! James and I know our duty to each other better, I pray Heaven!'

'Oh!' said Miss Dartle, nodding her head thoughtfully. 'To be sure. *That* would prevent it? Why, of course it would. Exactly. Now, I am glad I have been so foolish as to put the case, for it is so very good to know that your duty to each other would prevent it! Thank you very much.'

Later that evening I went with Steerforth into his room to say Good night.

'I shall be gone before you wake in the morning,' I said. 'Good night, my dear Steerforth.'

He was unwilling to let me go; and stood, holding me out, with a hand on each of my shoulders, as he had done in my own room.

'Daisy,' he said with a smile – 'for though that's not the name your godfathers and godmothers gave you, it's the name I like best to call you by – Daisy, if anything should ever separate us, you must think of me at my best, old boy. Come! Let us make that bargain. If circumstances should ever part us, think of me at my best.'

We shook hands, and we parted.

I was up with the dull dawn, and, having dressed as quietly as I could, looked into his room. He was fast asleep; lying, easily, with his head upon his arm, as I had often seen him lie at school.

The time came in its season, and that was very soon, when I almost wondered that nothing troubled his repose, as I looked at him, but he slept – let me think of him so again – as I had often seen him sleep at school; and thus, in this silent hour, I left him. Never more, oh God forgive you, Steerforth! to touch that passive hand in love and friendship. Never, never more!

28

I got down to Yarmouth in the evening. I knew that Peggotty's spare room – my room – was likely to have occupation enough in a little while, if that great Visitor, before whose presence all the living must give place, were not already in the house; so I betook myself to the inn, and dined there, and engaged my bed.

It was ten o'clock when I went out and directed my steps to the house.

My low tap at the door was answered by Mr Peggotty. He was not so much surprised to see me as I had expected. I remarked this in Peggotty, too, when she came down. In the expectation of that dread surprise, all other changes and surprises dwindle into nothing.

I shook hands with Mr Peggotty, and passed into the kitchen, while he softly closed the door. Little Emily was sitting by the fire, with her hands before her face. Ham was standing near her.

'Em'ly, my dear,' cried Mr Peggotty. 'See here! Here's Mas'r

Davy come! What, cheer up, pretty! Not a word to Mas'r Davy?'

There was a trembling upon her, that I can see now. The coldness of her hand when I touched it, I can feel yet.

'It's such a loving art,' said Mr Peggotty, smoothing her rich hair with his great hard hand, 'that it can't abear the sorrer of this. It's getting late, my dear, and here's Ham come fur to take you home. Theer! Go along with t'other loving art! What, Em'ly? Eh, my pretty?'

The sound of her voice had not reached me, but he bent his head as if he listened to her.

'You doesn't mean to ask me that! Stay with your uncle, Moppet? When your husband that'll be so soon is here fur to take you home?'

'Lookee here!' said Ham. 'As Em'ly wishes of it, I'll leave her till morning. Let me stay too!'

'No, no,' said Mr Peggotty. 'You go home and turn in. You ain't afeerd of Em'ly not being took good care on, *I* know.'

Ham yielded to this persuasion, and took his hat to go. Even when he kissed her she seemed to cling closer to her uncle, even to the avoidance of her chosen husband. I shut the door after him, that it might cause no disturbance of the quiet that prevailed.

'Now, I'm a going upstairs to tell your aunt as Mas'r Davy's here, and that'll cheer her up a bit,' he said.

When Peggotty came down she took me in her arms, and blessed and thanked me over and over again for being such a comfort to her in her distress. She then entreated me to come upstairs, sobbing that Mr Barkis had always liked me and admired me; and that he had often talked of me, before he fell into a stupor.

'Barkis, my dear!' said Peggotty, bending over him, while her brother and I stood at the bed's foot. 'Here's my dear boy – my dear boy, Master Davy, who brought us together, Barkis! That you sent messages by, you know! Won't you speak to Master Davy?'

'He's a going out with the tide,' said Mr Peggotty to me, behind his hand. 'People can't die, along the coast, except when the tide's pretty nigh out. They can't be born, not properly born, till flood. He's a going out with the tide.'

We remained there, watching him, a long time – hours. What mysterious influence my presence had upon him in that state of his senses, I shall not pretend to say; but when he at last began to wander feebly, it is certain he was muttering about driving me to school.

'Barkis, my dear!' said Peggotty.

'C. P. Barkis,' he said. 'No better woman anywhere!'

'Look! Here's Master Davy!' said Peggotty. For he now opened his eyes.

I was on the point of asking him if he knew me, when

he tried to stretch out his arm, and said to me, distinctly, with a pleasant smile:

'Barkis is willin'!'

And, it being low water, he went out with the tide.

29

It was not difficult for me, on Peggotty's solicitation, to resolve to stay where I was, until after the remains of the poor carrier should have made their last journey to Blunderstone.

In keeping Peggotty company, I had a supreme satisfaction in taking charge of Mr Barkis's will. He had hoarded, all these years, I found, to good purpose. His property in money amounted to nearly three thousand pounds. Of this he bequeathed the interest of one thousand to Mr Peggotty for his life; on his decease, the principal to be equally divided between Peggotty, little Emily, and me. All the rest he died possessed of, he bequeathed to Peggotty. In making an account for Peggotty of all the property into which she had come, in arranging all the affairs in an orderly manner, I passed the week before the funeral. I did not see little Emily in that interval, but they told me she was to be married in a fortnight.

I did not attend the funeral dressed up in a black coat and a streamer, to frighten the birds; but I walked over to

Blunderstone early in the morning, and was in the church-yard when it came, attended only by Peggotty and her brother.

My old nurse was to go to London with me next day on the business of the will, so we were all to meet in the old boathouse that night. Ham would bring Emily at the usual hour.

When I went in it looked very comfortable indeed. Mr Peggotty had smoked his evening pipe, the fire was bright, the locker was ready for little Emily in her old place. In her own old place sat Peggotty, once more, looking as if she had never left it. Mrs Gummidge appeared to be fretting a little, in her old corner; and consequently looked quite natural, too.

'You're first of the lot, Mas'r Davy!' said Mr Peggotty with a happy face.

He glanced at the Dutch clock, trimmed the candle, and put it in the window.

'Theer!' said Mr Peggotty. 'Lighted up, accordin' to custom! You're a wonderin' what that's fur, aren't you, sir! It's fur our little Em'ly. You see, the path ain't over light or cheerful after dark; and when I'm here at the hour as she's a comin' home, I puts the light in the winder. And here she is!'

It was only Ham.

'Wheer's Em'ly?' said Mr Peggotty.

Ham made a motion with his head, as if she were outside.

'Mas'r Davy, will you come out a minute, and see what Em'ly and me's got to show you?'

We went out. As I passed him at the door, I saw, to my astonishment and fright, that he was deadly pale. He pushed me hastily into the open air, and closed the door upon us. Only upon us two.

'Ham! What's the matter? For Heaven's sake, tell me what's the matter!'

'Mas'r Davy, the pride and hope of my art – her that I'd have died for, and would die for now – she's gone!'

'Gone!'

'Em'ly's run away! Oh, Mas'r Davy, what am I to say, in-doors? How am I ever to break it to him, Mas'r Davy?'

I saw the door move, and instinctively tried to hold the latch on the outside, to gain a moment's time. It was too late. Mr Peggotty thrust forth his face; and never could I forget the change that came upon it when he saw us, if I were to live five hundred years.

I remember a great wail and cry, and the women hanging about him, and we all standing in the room; I with a paper in my hand, which Ham had given me; Mr Peggotty, his hair wild, his face and lips quite white, looking fixedly at me.

'Read it, sir,' he said. 'Slow, please. I doen't know as I can understand.'

In the midst of the silence of death, I read thus, from a blotted letter.

'"When you, who love me so much better than I have ever deserved, see this, I shall be far away. When I leave my dear home in the morning,"' the letter bore date on the previous night:

'" – it will be never to come back, unless he brings me back a lady. I am too wicked to write about myself. Take comfort in thinking that. For mercy's sake, tell uncle that I never loved him half so dear as now. Don't remember we were ever to be married – but try to think as if I died when I was little. Love some good girl that will be what I was once to uncle, and be true to you, and worthy of you. God bless all! I'll pray for all, often, on my knees. My parting love to uncle. My last tears, and my last thanks, for uncle!"'

That was all.

He stood, long after I had ceased to read, still looking at me. Then he said:

'Who's the man? I want to know his name.'

Ham glanced at me, and suddenly I felt a shock that struck me back.

'Mas'r Davy!' implored Ham. 'Go out a bit, and let me tell him what I must. You doen't ought to hear it, sir.'

I sank down in a chair, and tried to utter some reply; but my tongue was fettered.

'I want to know his name!' I heard said once more.

'For some time past,' said Ham, 'there's been a servant about here, at odd times. There's been a gen'lm'n too. Both of 'em belonged to one another.'

Mr Peggotty stood fixed as before.

'The servant,' pursued Ham, 'was seen along with – our poor girl – last night. He's been hiding about here, this week or over. A strange chay and hosses was outside town, this morning, on the Norwich road, a'most afore the day broke. Em'ly was nigh him. The t'other was inside. He's the man.'

'For the Lord's love,' said Mr Peggotty. 'Don't tell me his name's Steerforth!'

'Mas'r Davy,' said Ham, 'it ain't no fault of yourn but his name is Steerforth, and he's a damned villain!'

Mr Peggotty pulled down his rough coat from its peg in a corner.

Ham asked him whither he was going.

'I'm a going to seek my niece. I'm a going to seek my Em'ly. I'm a going, first to stave in that theer boat, and sink it. Then I'm a going to seek my niece through the wureld. I'm a going to find my poor niece in her shame, and bring her back. No one stop me!'

30

In the morning I was joined by Mr Peggotty and my old nurse, and we went at an early hour to the coach office.

When we got to our journey's end, our first pursuit was to look about for a little lodging for Peggotty, where her brother could have a bed. We were fortunate to find one over a chandler's shop, only two streets removed from me.

Mr Peggotty had made a communication to me on the way to London, for which I was not unprepared. It was, that he proposed first seeing Mrs Steerforth. With a view of sparing the mother's feelings as much as possible, I wrote to her that night. I told her as mildly as I could what his wrong was. I said he was a man in very common life, but of a most gentle and upright character; and I ventured to hope that she would not refuse to see him in his heavy trouble. I mentioned two o'clock in the afternoon as the hour of our coming, and I sent the letter myself by the first coach in the morning.

At the appointed time, we stood at the door.

No Littimer appeared. The pleasanter face of the parlour-maid answered to our summons, and went before us to the drawing-room. Mrs Steerforth was sitting there. Rosa Dartle glided, as we went in, from another part of the room, and stood behind her chair.

I saw, directly, in his mother's face, that she knew from himself what he had done.

She sat upright in her arm-chair and looked very stead-fastly at Mr Peggotty when he stood before her; and he looked, quite as steadfastly, at her.

She motioned to Mr Peggotty to be seated. He said:

'I shouldn't feel it nat'ral, ma'am, to sit down in this house. I'd sooner stand.'

'I know, with deep regret, what has brought you here,' she said. 'What do you want of me? What do you ask me to do?'

Feeling in his breast for Emily's letter, he took it out and gave it to her.

'Please to read that, ma'am. That's my niece's hand!'

She read it, in the same stately and impassive way, and returned it to him.

'"Unless he brings me back a lady,"' said Mr Peggotty, tracing out that part with his finger. 'I come to know, ma'am, whether he will keep his wured.'

'No.'

'Why not?' said Mr Peggotty.

'It is impossible. He would disgrace himself. You cannot fail to know that she is far below him.'

'Raise her up!' said Mr Peggotty.

'I am sorry to repeat, it is impossible. Such a marriage would irretrievably blight my son's career, and ruin his prospects. Nothing is more certain than that it never can take place, and never will. If there is any other compensation . . .'

'Money?' said Mr Peggotty. 'For my child's blight and ruin?'

She changed now, in a moment. An angry flush overspread her features.

'And what compensation can you make to *me* for opening such a pit between me and my son? My son, who has been the object of my life, to whom its every thought has been devoted – to take up in a moment with a miserable girl, and avoid me! To repay my confidence with systematic deception, for her sake, and quit me for her! Is this no injury?'

She rose to leave the room, when Mr Peggotty signified that it was needless.

'I have no more to say, ma'am,' he remarked, as he moved towards the door. 'I come heer with no hope, and I take away no hope. I have done what I thowt should be done.'

With this, we departed; leaving her standing by her elbow-chair, a picture of a noble presence and a handsome face.

We went back to the little lodging over the chandler's shop, and we all three dined together off a beefsteak pie. After dinner we sat for an hour or so near the window, without talking much; and then Mr Peggotty got up, and brought his oilskin bag and his stout stick, and laid them on the table.

He accepted, from his sister's stock of ready money, a small sum on account of his legacy; barely enough, I should have thought, to keep him for a month. He slung his bag about him and took his hat and stick.

'All good attend you, dear old woman,' he said, embracing Peggotty, 'and you too, Mas'r Davy!' shaking hands with me. 'I'm a going to seek her, fur and wide. If any hurt should come to me, remember that the last words I left for her was, "My unchanged love is with my darling child, and I forgive her!"' Then, putting on his hat, he went down the stairs, and away.

31

All this time, I had gone on loving Dora, harder than ever. The more I pitied myself, or pitied others, the more I sought for consolation in the image of Dora.

My love was so much in my mind, and it was so natural to me to confide in Peggotty, that I imparted to her, in a sufficiently roundabout way, my great secret. Peggotty was strongly interested, but I could not get her into my view of the case at all. She was audaciously prejudiced in my favour, and quite unable to understand why I should have any misgivings, or be low-spirited about it.

'The young lady might think herself well off,' she observed, 'to have such a beau. And as to her pa, what *did* the gentleman expect, for gracious sake!'

This I was soon to discover, for the following day, Mr Spenlow and I falling into conversation, it came about that Mr Spenlow told me this day week was Dora's birthday, and he would be glad if I would come down and join a little picnic on the occasion. I went out of my senses immediately and passed the intervening period in a state of dotage.

I think I committed every possible absurdity in the way of preparation for this blessed event. On the day, at six in the morning, I was in Covent Garden Market, buying a bouquet for Dora. At ten I was on horseback with the bouquet in my hat, to keep it fresh, trotting down to Norwood.

When I saw Dora on a garden-seat under a lilac tree, what a spectacle she was, upon that beautiful morning, among the butterflies.

There was a young lady with her – comparatively stricken in years – almost twenty, I should say. Her name was Miss Mills, and Dora called her Julia. She was the bosom friend of Dora. Happy Miss Mills!

Her dog Jip was there, and Jip *would* bark at me. When I presented my bouquet, he gnashed his teeth with jealousy. Well he might. If he had the least idea how I adored his mistress, well he might!

'Oh, thank you, Mr Copperfield! What dear flowers!' said Dora.

She held my flowers to Jip to smell. Jip growled, and wouldn't smell them. Then Dora laughed.

'You'll be so glad to hear, Mr Copperfield, that that cross Miss Murdstone is not here. She will be away at least three weeks. Isn't that delightful?'

I said I was sure it must be delightful to her, and all that was delightful to her was delightful to me. Miss Mills, with an air of superior wisdom and benevolence, smiled upon us.

But now Mr Spenlow came out of the house, and we all walked from the lawn towards the carriage.

I shall never have such a ride again. I never have had such another. Dora sat with her back to the horses, looking towards me. She kept the bouquet close to her on the cushion, and often refreshed herself with its fragrance. Our eyes at those times often met; and my great astonishment is that I didn't go over the head of my gallant grey into the carriage.

Mr Spenlow stood up sometimes, and asked me what I thought of the prospect. I said it was delightful, and I dare say it was; but it was all Dora to me.

I don't know to this hour where we went. Perhaps it was near Guildford. It was a green spot, on a hill, carpeted with soft turf. There were shady trees, and heather, and, as far as the eye could see, a rich landscape.

It was a trying thing to find people here, waiting for us.

We all unpacked our baskets, and employed ourselves in getting dinner ready.

I have but an indistinct idea of what happened. I was very merry, I know. Dora's health was drunk. I caught Dora's eye as I bowed to her, and I thought it looked appealing.

When the party broke up, and the other people went their several ways, we went ours through the still evening and the dying light, with sweet scents rising up around us. Mr Spenlow being a little drowsy after the champagne and being fast asleep in a corner of the carriage, I rode by the side and talked to Dora. She admired my horse and patted him – oh, what a dear little hand it looked upon a horse! – and her shawl would not keep right, and now and then I drew it round her with my arm.

Then that sagacious Miss Mills; what a kind thing *she* did!

'Mr Copperfield,' said Miss Mills, 'Dora is coming to stay with me. She is coming home with me the day after to-morrow. If you would like to call, I am sure papa would be happy to see you.'

What could I do but invoke a silent blessing on Miss Mills's head?

When I awoke next morning, I was resolute to declare my passion to Dora, and know my fate. I passed three days in a luxury of wretchedness. At last, arrayed for the purpose at a vast expense, I went to Miss Mills's, fraught with a declaration.

I was shown into a room upstairs, where Miss Mills and Dora were. Jip was there.

Miss Mills was very glad to see me, and very sorry her papa was not at home: though I thought we all bore that with fortitude. Miss Mills was conversational for a few minutes, and then got up and left the room.

I don't know how I did it. I did it in a moment. I had Dora in my arms. I was full of eloquence. I never stopped for a word. I told her how I loved her. I told her I should die without her. I told her that I idolized and worshipped her. Jip barked madly all the time.

Well, well! Dora and I were sitting on the sofa by and by, quiet enough, and Jip was lying in her lap, winking peacefully at me. It was off my mind and I was in a state of perfect rapture. Dora and I were engaged.

32

I wrote to Agnes a long letter, in which I tried to make her comprehend how blest I was, and what a darling Dora was. I entreated Agnes not to regard this as a thoughtless passion which could ever yield to any other.

Of Steerforth I said nothing. I only told her there had been sad grief at Yarmouth, on account of Emily's flight.

While I had been away from home, Traddles had called twice or thrice. Finding Peggotty within, he had established a good-humoured acquaintance with her, and had stayed to have a little chat with her about me.

This reminds me, not only that I expected Traddles on a certain afternoon of his own appointing, which was now come, but that Mrs Crupp had resigned everything appertaining to her office (the salary excepted) until Peggotty should cease to present herself. Mrs Crupp, after holding divers conversations respecting Peggotty, in a very high-pitched voice, on the staircase – with some invisible Familiar, for she was quite alone – addressed a letter to me, developing her views.

After this, Mrs Crupp confined herself to making pitfalls on the stairs, principally with pitchers, and endeavouring to delude Peggotty into breaking her legs.

I found it rather harassing to live in this state of siege, but was much too afraid of Mrs Crupp to see any way out of it.

'My dear Copperfield,' cried Traddles, punctually appearing at my door, in spite of all these obstacles, 'how do you do?'

'My dear Traddles,' I said, 'I am delighted to see you at last. And how is Mr Micawber?'

'He is quite well, Copperfield, thank you,' said Traddles. 'I am not living with him at present.'

'No?'

'No. You see the truth is, he has changed his name to Mortimer, in consequence of his temporary embarrassments; and he don't come out till after dark – and then in spectacles. There was an execution put into our house, for rent. Mrs Micawber was in such a dreadful state that I really couldn't resist giving my name to a bill. The broker carried off my little round table with the marble top, and Sophy's flower-pot and stand.'

'What a hard thing!' I exclaimed indignantly.

'It was a – it was a pull,' said Traddles. 'The fact is, Copperfield, I was unable to repurchase them at the time of their seizure, but I have kept my eye upon the broker's shop. Today I find them put out for sale. What has occurred to me, having now the money, is that perhaps you wouldn't object to ask that good nurse of yours to come with me to the shop and make the best bargain for them, as if they were for herself.'

I told him that my old nurse would be delighted to assist him, but on condition that he grant no more loans of his name, or anything else, to Mr Micawber.

He went round to the chandler's shop, to enlist Peggotty.

I never shall forget him peeping round the corner of the street in Tottenham Court Road, while Peggotty was bargaining for the precious articles; or his agitation when she came slowly towards us after vainly offering a price, and was hailed by the relenting broker, and went back again. The end of the negotiation was, that she bought the property on tolerably easy terms, and Traddles was transported with pleasure.

Peggotty and I turned back towards my chambers.

On our way upstairs, we were both very much surprised to find my outer door standing open (which I had shut), and to hear voices inside.

What was my amazement to find, of all people upon earth, my aunt there, and Mr Dick! My aunt sitting on a quantity of luggage, with her two birds before her, and her cat on her knee, like a female Robinson Crusoe, drinking tea. Mr Dick leaning thoughtfully on a great kite, such as we had often been out together to fly, and with more luggage piled about him!

'My dear aunt!' I cried. 'Why, what an unexpected pleasure!'

We cordially embraced; and Mr Dick and I cordially shook hands; and Mrs Crupp, who was busy making tea, and could not be too attentive, cordially said she had knowed well as Mr Copperfull would have his heart in his mouth, when he see his dear relations.

'Holloa!' said my aunt to Peggotty, who quailed before her awful presence. 'What's your name now?'

'Barkis, ma'am,' said Peggotty, with a curtsey.

'Well! That's human,' said my aunt. 'It sounds less as if you wanted a missionary. How d'ye do, Barkis? I hope you're well?'

Here my aunt looked hard at Mrs Crupp. 'We needn't trouble you to wait, ma'am.'

'Shall I put a little more tea in the pot afore I go, ma'am?' said Mrs Crupp.

'No, I thank you, ma'am,' replied my aunt.

Mrs Crupp, who had been incessantly smiling to express sweet temper, gradually smiled herself out of the room.

I knew my aunt sufficiently well to know that she had something of importance on her mind. I began to reflect whether I had done anything to offend her; and my conscience whispered me that I had not yet told her about Dora. Could it by any means be that, I wondered!

'Trot,' said my aunt at last, when she had finished her tea, 'you needn't go, Barkis! – Trot, have you got to be firm and self-reliant?'

'I think so, aunt.'

'Then, my love,' said my aunt, looking earnestly at me, 'why do you think I sit upon this property of mine tonight?'

I shook my head, unable to guess.

'Because,' said my aunt, 'it's all I have. Because I'm ruined, my dear!'

If the house, and every one of us, had tumbled out into the river together, I could hardly have received a greater shock.

'Dick knows it,' said my aunt, laying her hand calmly on my shoulder. 'I am ruined, my dear Trot! All I have in the world is in this room, except the cottage; and that I have left Janet to let. Barkis, I want to get a bed for this gentleman tonight. To save expense, perhaps you can make something up here for myself. Anything will do. It's only for tonight. We'll talk about this, more, to-morrow.'

33

As soon as I could recover my presence of mind, I proposed to Mr Dick to come round to the chandler's shop, and take possession of the bed which Mr Peggotty had lately vacated.

My aunt was walking up and down the room when I returned, crimping the borders of her nightcap with her fingers. I warmed some ale, which she insisted on in place of wine, to save expense, and made the toast on the usual infallible principles. When it was ready for her, she was ready for it.

'My dear,' said my aunt, after taking a spoonful of ale; 'it's a great deal better than wine. Not half so bilious.'

I suppose I looked doubtful, for she added:

'Tut, tut, child. If nothing worse than Ale happens to us, we are well off.'

My aunt went on with a quiet enjoyment, drinking the warm ale with a teaspoon, and soaking her strips of toast in it.

'Trot,' she said, 'I don't care for strange faces in general, but I rather like that Barkis of yours, do you know!'

'It's better than a hundred pounds to hear you say so!'

'Barkis is uncommonly fond of you, Trot.'

'There is nothing she would leave undone to prove it,' I said.

'Nothing, I believe,' returned my aunt. 'Here, the poor fool has been begging and praying about handing over some of her money – because she has got too much of it. A simpleton!'

My aunt's tears of pleasure were positively trickling down into the warm ale.

'I know all about it, Trot! Barkis and myself had quite a gossip while you were out with Dick. I know all about it. I don't know where these wretched girls expect to go to.'

'Poor Emily!' I said.

'Oh, don't talk to me about poor,' returned my aunt. 'She should have thought of that before she caused so much misery! Give me a kiss, Trot. I am sorry for your early experience.'

As I bent forward, she put her tumbler on my knee to detain me, and said:

'Oh, Trot, Trot! And so you fancy yourself in love! Do you?'

'Fancy, aunt!' I exclaimed, as red as I could be. 'I adore her with my whole soul!'

'Dora, indeed!' returned my aunt. 'And so you think you were formed for one another, and are to go through a party-supper-table kind of life, like two pretty pieces of confectionery, do you, Trot?'

She asked me this so kindly, that I was quite touched.

'I dare say we say and think a good deal that is rather foolish. But we love one another truly, I am sure.'

'Well,' said my aunt, 'I don't want to put two young creatures out of conceit with themselves, or to make them unhappy; so, we'll hope for a prosperous issue one of these days.'

This was not upon the whole very comforting to a rapturous lover; but I was glad to have my aunt in my confidence. So I thanked her ardently for this mark of her affection, and for all her other kindnesses towards me; and after a tender goodnight, she took her nightcap into my bedroom.

On the following day, as I made my way homeward from the office, a hackney-chariot coming after me, and stopping at my very feet, occasioned me to look up. A fair hand was stretched forth to me from the window; and the face I had never seen without a feeling of serenity and happiness, was smiling on me.

'Agnes!' I exclaimed. 'Oh, my dear Agnes, of all the people in the world, what a pleasure to see you! Where are you going?'

She was going to my rooms to see my aunt.

My aunt had written her one of her odd, abrupt notes, stating that she had fallen into adversity, and was leaving Dover for good. Agnes had come to London to see her.

She was not alone, she said. Her papa was with her – and Uriah Heep.

'And now they are partners,' I said. 'Confound him!'

'Yes,' said Agnes. 'They have some business here; and I took advantage of their coming, to come too. I do not like to let papa go away alone, with him.'

'Does he exercise the same influence over Mr Wickfield still, Agnes?'

'There is such a change at home,' she said, 'that you would scarcely know the dear old house. They live with us now.'

'They?'

'Mr Heep and his mother.'

We found my aunt alone, and began to talk about my aunt's losses.

'Now, Trot and Agnes,' she said, 'let us look the case of Betsey Trotwood in the face, and see how it stands.'

My aunt, patting her cat, looked very attentively at Agnes.

'Betsey Trotwood,' said my aunt, who had always kept her money matters to herself: 'had a certain security that did very well, and returned very good interest, till Betsey was paid off. Then, Betsey had to look about her, for a new investment. She thought she was wiser, now, than her man of business, who was not such a good man of business by this time as he used to be – I am alluding to your father, Agnes – and she took it into her head to lay it out for herself. So she took her pigs to a foreign market; and a very bad market it turned out to be. It fell to pieces, and never will and never can pay sixpence; and Betsey's sixpences were all there, and there's an end of them. Least said, soonest mended!'

Agnes had listened at first with suspended breath. Her colour still came and went, but she breathed more freely. I thought I knew why. I thought she had had some fear that her unhappy father might be in some way to blame for what had happened. My aunt took her hand in hers, and laughed.

'What's to be done? Here's the cottage will produce, say, seventy pounds a year. That's all we've got. There's Dick. He's good for a hundred a year, but of course that must be expended on himself. How can Trot and I do best, upon our means? What do you say, Agnes?'

'I say, aunt,' I interposed, 'that I must do something!'

'I have been thinking, Trotwood,' said Agnes, diffidently, 'that if you had time . . .'

'I have a good deal of time, Agnes. I am always disengaged after four or five o'clock, and I have time early in the morning.'

'I know you would not mind,' said Agnes, coming to me, 'the duties of a secretary.'

'Mind, my dear Agnes?'

'Because,' continued Agnes, 'Doctor Strong has acted on his intention of retiring, and has come to live in London; and he asked papa, I know, if he could recommend him one. Don't you think he would rather have his favourite old pupil near him, than anybody else?'

'Dear Agnes!' said I. 'What should I do without you! You are always my good angel. I told you so. I never think of you in any other light.'

Agnes answered with her pleasant laugh, and was saying that one good angel (meaning Dora) was enough, when a knock came at the door.

'I think,' said Agnes, 'it's papa. He promised me that he would come.'

I opened the door, and admitted, not only Mr Wickfield, but Uriah Heep.

I had not seen Mr Wickfield for some time. I was prepared for a great change in him, but his appearance shocked me. It was not that he looked many years older, or that there was a nervous trembling in his hand, but the thing that struck me most was that he should submit himself to that crawling impersonation of meanness, Uriah Heep. The reversal of the two natures, in their relative positions, Uriah's of power and Mr Wickfield's of dependence, was a sight more painful to me than I can express.

'Well, Wickfield!' said my aunt; 'I have been telling your daughter how well I have been disposing of my money for myself, because I couldn't trust it to you, as you were growing rusty in business matters. We have been taking counsel together, and getting along very well, all things considered. Agnes is worth the whole firm, in my opinion.'

'If I may umbly make the remark,' said Uriah Heep, with a writhe, 'I fully agree with Miss Betsey Trotwood, and should be only too appy if Miss Agnes was a partner. And you, Master – I should say, Mister Copperfield,' pursued Uriah, 'I am rejoiced to see you, even under present circumstances which is not what your friends would wish for you, Mister Copperfield, but it isn't money makes the man. I am bespoke on business, otherwise I should have been appy to have kept with my friends. But I leave my partner to represent the firm. Miss Agnes, ever yours! I wish you good-day, Master Copperfield, and leave my umble respects for Miss Betsey Trotwood.'

With these words, he retired, kissing his great hand, and leering at us like a mask.

34

I was pretty busy now; up at five in the morning, and home at nine or ten at night. But I had infinite satisfaction in being so closely engaged, and felt enthusiastically that the more I tired myself, the more I was doing to deserve Dora.

Not satisfied with all these proceedings, but burning with impatience to do something more, I went to see Traddles.

The first subject on which I had to consult Traddles was this: I had heard that many men, distinguished in various pursuits, had begun life by reporting the debates in Parliament. I told Traddles that I wished to know how I could qualify myself for this pursuit.

Traddles informed me that the mechanical acquisition of a perfect and entire command of the mystery of short-hand writing and reading was about equal in difficulty to the mastery of six languages.

'I am very much obliged to you, my dear Traddles!' I said. 'I'll begin to-morrow.'

And we went off together to the lodging which Mr

Micawber occupied as Mr Mortimer, and which was situated near the top of Gray's Inn Road.

'My dear Copperfield,' said Mr Micawber, 'yourself and Mr Traddles find us on the brink of migration, and will excuse any little discomforts incidental to that position.'

Glancing round as I made a suitable reply, I observed that the family effects were already packed, and that the amount of luggage was by no means overwhelming. I congratulated Mrs Micawber on the approaching change.

'My dear Mr Copperfield,' said Mrs Micawber, 'my family may consider it banishment, if they please; but I am a wife and mother, and I never will desert Mr Micawber. It may be a sacrifice to immure oneself in a Cathedral town; but surely, Mr Copperfield, if it is a sacrifice in me, it is much more a sacrifice in a man of Mr Micawber's abilities.'

'Oh! You are going to a Cathedral town?' I said.

'To Canterbury,' said Mr Micawber. 'In fact, my dear Copperfield, I have entered into arrangements, by virtue of which I stand pledged and contracted, to our friend Heep, to assist and serve him in the capacity of his confidential clerk.'

I stared at Mr Micawber, who greatly enjoyed my surprise.

'Of my friend Heep,' said Mr Micawber, 'who is a man of remarkable shrewdness, I desire to speak with all possible respect. My friend Heep has not fixed the positive remuneration at too high a figure, but such address and intelligence as I chance to possess, will be devoted to my friend Heep's service.'

'What I particularly request Mr Micawber to be careful of, is,' said Mrs Micawber, 'that he does not, my dear Mr Copperfield, in applying himself to this subordinate branch of the law, place it out of his power to rise, ultimately, to the top of the tree – a Judge, or even say a Chancellor.'

'My dear,' observed Mr Micawber, 'we have time enough before us, for the consideration of these questions.'

'Micawber,' she returned, 'no! Your mistake in life is, that you do not look forward far enough. You are bound, in justice to your family, if not to yourself, to take in, at a comprehensive glance, the extremest point in the horizon to which your abilities may lead you.'

My Micawber coughed, and I quite believe that he saw himself, in his judicial mind's eye, on the woolsack.

'It is my intention, my dear Copperfield, to educate my son for the Church; I will not deny that I should be happy, on his account, to attain to eminence.'

'For the Church?' I said, still pondering, between whiles, on Uriah Heep.

'Yes,' said Mr Micawber. 'He has a remarkable head-voice, and will commence as a chorister. Our residence at Canterbury, and our local connection, will, no doubt, enable him to take advantage of any vacancy that may arise in the Cathedral corps.'

On looking at Master Micawber, I saw that he had a

certain expression of face, as if his voice were behind his eyebrows.

'One thing more I have to do, before this separation is complete,' said Mr Micawber, 'and that is to perform an act of justice. My friend Mr Thomas Traddles has, on two several occasions, "put his name", if I may use a common expression, to bills of exchange for my accommodation. These sums, united, make a total, if my calculation is correct, amounting to forty-one, ten, eleven and a half . . .

'To leave this metropolis, without acquitting myself of the pecuniary part of this obligation, would weigh upon my mind to an insupportable extent. I have, therefore, prepared and I now hold in my hand, a document, which accomplishes the desired object. I beg to hand to my friend Mr Thomas Traddles my I.O.U. for forty-one, ten, eleven and a half, and I am happy to recover my moral dignity, and to know that I can once more walk erect before my fellow man!'

With this introduction (which greatly affected him), Mr Micawber placed his I.O.U. in the hands of Traddles and said he wished him well in every relation of life. I am persuaded, not only that this was quite the same to Mr Micawber as paying the money, but that Traddles himself hardly knew the difference until he had had time to think about it. Mr Micawber walked so erect before his fellow men on the strength of this virtuous action, that his chest looked half as broad again when he lighted us downstairs.

We parted with great heartiness on both sides, and when I had seen Traddles to his own door, and was going home alone, I thought, among the other odd and contradictory things I mused upon, that, slippery as Mr Micawber was, I was probably indebted to some compassionate recollection he retained of me as his boy lodger, for never having been asked by him for money. I certainly should not have had the moral courage to refuse it, and I have no doubt he knew that, quite as well as I did.

35

I did not allow my resolution, with respect to the Parliamentary Debates, to cool. I bought an approved scheme of the noble art and mystery of stenography (which cost me ten and sixpence); and plunged into a sea of perplexity that brought me, in a few weeks, the confines of distraction. The changes that were rung upon dots, the wonderful vagaries that were played by circles; the tremendous effects of a curve in a wrong place; not only troubled my waking hours, but re-appeared before me in my sleep.

I resorted to Traddles for advice; who suggested that he should dictate speeches to me, at a pace, and with occasional stoppages, adapted to my weakness. And so, night after night, we had a sort of Private Parliament in Buckingham Street, after I came home from the Doctor's.

I should like to see such a Parliament anywhere else! My aunt and Mr Dick represented the Government or the Opposition (as the case might be), and Traddles, as Mr Pitt, Mr Fox, Lord Castlereagh, or Mr Canning, would deliver the most withering denunciations of the profligacy and corruption of my aunt and Mr Dick.

Often and often we pursued these debates until the clock pointed to midnight, and the candles were burning down. The result of so much good practice was that by and by I began to keep pace with Traddles pretty well. Yet I was always punctual at the office; at the Doctor's too: and I really did work, as the common expression is, like a cart-horse.

One day, when I went to the Commons as usual, I found Mr Spenlow in the doorway looking extremely grave.

Instead of returning my 'Good morning' with his usual affability, he coldly requested me to accompany him to a certain coffee-house. I complied, in a very uncomfortable state, and I could hardly have failed to know what was the matter when I followed him into an upstairs room, and found Miss Murdstone there.

Miss Murdstone gave me her chilly finger-nails, and sat severely rigid. Mr Spenlow shut the door, motioned me to a chair, and stood on the hearth-rug in front of the fireplace.

'Have the goodness to show Mr Copperfield,' said Mr Spenlow, 'what you have in your reticule, Miss Murdstone.'

Compressing her lips, Miss Murdstone produced my last letter to Dora, teeming with expressions of devoted affection.

'I believe that is your writing, Mr Copperfield?' said Mr Spenlow.

The voice I heard was very unlike mine.

'It is, sir!'

'If I am not mistaken,' said Mr Spenlow, as Miss Murd-stone brought a parcel of letters out of her reticule, tied round with the dearest bit of blue ribbon, 'those are also from your pen, Mr Copperfield?'

I took them from her with a most desolate sensation; blushed deeply, and inclined my head.

'Miss Murdstone, be so good as to proceed!'

'Last evening after tea,' said Miss Murdstone, 'I observed the little dog growling about the drawing-room, worrying something. The dog retreated under the sofa on my approaching him, and was with great difficulty dislodged by the fire-irons. Even when dislodged, he still kept the letter in his mouth. At length I obtained possession of it. After perusing it, I taxed Miss Spenlow with having many such letters in her possession; and ultimately obtained from her the packet which is now in David Copperfield's hand.'

Mr Spenlow turned to me. 'I beg to ask, Mr Copperfield, if you have anything to say?'

The picture I had before me, of the beautiful little treasure of my heart, sobbing and crying all night, very much impaired the little dignity I had been able to muster.

'There is nothing I can say, sir,' I returned, 'except that all the blame is mine. Dora . . .'

'Miss Spenlow, if you please,' said her father, majestically.

'. . . was induced and persuaded by me to consent to this concealment, and I bitterly regret it.'

'You are very much to blame, sir,' said Mr Spenlow, walking to and fro upon the hearth-rug. 'When I take a gentleman to my house, no matter whether he is nineteen, twenty-nine, or ninety, I take him there in a spirit of confidence. If he abuses my confidence, he commits a dishonourable action, Mr Copperfield.'

'I feel it, sir, I assure you,' I said. 'But I never thought so, before. I love Miss Spenlow to that extent . . .'

'Pooh! nonsense!' said Mr Spenlow, reddening. 'Pray don't tell me to my face that you love my daughter, Mr Copperfield! Let there be an end of the nonsense. Take away those letters, and throw them in the fire; and although our future intercourse must be restricted to the Commons here, we will agree to make no further mention of the past. Come, Mr Copperfield, this is the sensible course.'

No. I couldn't think of agreeing to it. I was very sorry, but there was a higher consideration than sense. Love was above all earthly considerations, and I loved Dora, and Dora loved me. I softened it down as much as I could; but I was resolute upon it.

'Very well, Mr Copperfield,' said Mr Spenlow, 'I must try my influence with my daughter.'

I confided all to my aunt when I got home; and in spite of all she could say to me, went to bed despairing. I got up despairing, and went out despairing. It was Saturday morning, and I went straight to the Commons.

I was surprised, when I came within sight of our office-door, to see the ticket-porters standing there outside talking together, and some half-dozen stragglers gazing at the windows which were shut up. I quickened my pace, and went hurriedly in.

The clerks were there, but nobody was doing anything.

'This is a dreadful calamity, Mr Copperfield,' said old Tiffey, as I entered.

'What is it?' I exclaimed. 'What's the matter?'

'Don't you know?' cried Tiffey, and all the rest of them, coming round me.

'No!' said I, looking from face to face.

'Mr Spenlow,' said Tiffey.

'What about him!'

'Dead!'

I thought it was the office reeling, and not I, as one of the clerks caught hold of me. They sat me down in a chair, untied my neckcloth, and brought me some water.

I cannot describe the state of mind into which I was thrown by this intelligence. The shock of such an event happening so suddenly, and happening to one with whom I had been in any respect at variance, this is easily intelligible to anyone. What I cannot describe is how, in the innermost recesses of my own heart, I had a lurking jealousy even of Death. How I felt as if its might would push me from my ground in Dora's thoughts.

In the trouble of this state of mind, I got my aunt to address a letter to Miss Mills, which I wrote. I deplored the untimely death of Mr Spenlow, most sincerely. I entreated her to tell Dora, if Dora were in a state to hear it, that he had spoken to me with the utmost kindness and consideration; and had coupled her name with nothing but tenderness.

My aunt received a few lines next day in reply, addressed, outside, to her; within, to me. Dora was overcome by grief; and when her friend had asked her should she send her love to me, had only cried, as she was always crying, 'Oh, dear papa! oh, poor papa!' But she had not said No, and that I made the most of.

Mr Jorkins, the late Mr Spenlow's partner, came to the office a few days afterwards. He and Tiffey were closeted together for some few moments, and then Tiffey looked out at the door and beckoned me in.

'Mr Copperfield,' said Mr Jorkins, 'Mr Tiffey and myself are about to examine the desks and other such repositories of the deceased, with a view to searching for a will. There is no trace of any, elsewhere. It may be as well for you to assist us, if you please.'

We began the search at once and were going on dustily and quietly, when Mr Jorkins said to us, 'Mr Spenlow was very difficult to move from the beaten track. You know what he was! I am disposed to think he had made no will.'

It turned out that there *was* no will. He had never so much as thought of making one, so far as his papers afforded any evidence. What was scarcely less astonishing to me was that his affairs were in a most disordered state, and Tiffey told me, little thinking how interested I was in the story, that, paying all the debts of the deceased, he wouldn't give a thousand pounds for the assets remaining.

This was at the expiration of about six weeks. I had suffered tortures all the time, when Miss Mills still reported to me that my broken-hearted little Dora would say nothing, when I was mentioned, but 'Oh, poor papa! oh, dear papa!' Also, that she had no other relations than two aunts, maiden sisters of Mr Spenlow, who lived at Putney.

These two ladies now emerged from their retirement, and proposed to take Dora to live at Putney. Dora, clinging to them both, and weeping, exclaimed:

'Oh yes, aunts! please take Julia Mills and me and Jip to Putney!'

So they went, very soon after the funeral.

36

My aunt, beginning, I imagine, to be made seriously uncomfortable by my prolonged dejection, made a pretence of being anxious that I should go to Dover to see that all was working well at the cottage, which was let; and to conclude an agreement, with the same tenant, for a longer term of occupation.

I found everything in a satisfactory state at the cottage; and was enabled to gratify my aunt exceedingly by reporting that the tenant inherited her feud, and waged incessant war against donkeys. Having settled the little business I had to transact there, and slept there one night, I walked on to Canterbury early in the morning.

It was now winter again; and the fresh, cold windy day, and the sweeping downland, brightened up my hopes a little.

Arrived at Mr Wickfield's house, I found, in the little lower room on the ground-floor, where Uriah Heep had been of old accustomed to sit, Mr Micawber plying his pen with great assiduity. He was dressed in a legal-looking suit of black, and loomed, burly and large, in that small office.

'How do you like the law, Mr Micawber?' I said.

'My dear Copperfield,' he replied. 'To a man possessed of the higher imaginative powers, the objection to legal studies is the amount of detail which they involve. Still, it is a great pursuit. A great pursuit!'

He then told me that he had become the tenant of Uriah Heep's old house, and that Mrs Micawber would be delighted to receive me, once more, under her own roof.

'It is humble,' said Mr Micawber, '(to quote a favourite expression of my friend Heep), but it may prove the stepping-stone to more ambitious domiciliary accommodation.'

I asked him whether he had reason, so far, to be satisfied with his friend Heep's treatment of him? He got up to ascertain if the door were close shut, before he replied:

'My dear Copperfield, a man who labours under the pressure of pecuniary embarrassments is, with the generality of people, at a disadvantage. All I can say is, that my friend Heep has responded to appeals to which I need not more particularly refer, in a manner calculated to redound equally to the honour of his head, and of his heart.'

'I am glad your experience is so favourable,' I returned. 'And do you see much of Mr Wickfield?'

'Not much,' said Mr Micawber. 'Mr Wickfield is – in short, he is obsolete.'

'I am afraid his partner seeks to make him so,' I said.

'My dear Copperfield!' returned Mr Micawber, after some uneasy evolutions on his stool. 'I would take the liberty of suggesting that in our friendly intercourse – which I trust will never be disturbed – we draw a line. On one side of this line,' said Mr Micawber, representing it on the desk with the office ruler, 'is the whole range of the human intellect, with a trifling exception; on the other, *is* that exception – that is to say, the affairs of Messrs Wickfield and Heep. I trust I give no offence?'

I felt I had no right to be offended. My telling him so appeared to relieve him; and he shook hands with me.

I took my leave of Mr Micawber, and looked into the room still belonging to Agnes. I saw her sitting by the fire, at a pretty old-fashioned desk she had, writing.

My darkening the light made her look up. What a pleasure to be the cause of that bright change in her attentive face, and the object of that sweet regard and welcome!

'Oh, Agnes!' I said, when we were sitting together, side by side; 'I have missed you so much, lately!'

'Indeed?' she replied. 'Again! And so soon?'

In her placid sisterly manner, she soon led me on to tell all that had happened since our last meeting.

'What ought I to do, Agnes?' I enquired, after looking at the fire a little while. 'What would it be right to do?'

'I think,' said Agnes, 'that the honourable course to take, would be to write to those two ladies.'

With a lightened heart, though with a profound sense of the weighty importance of my task, I devoted the whole afternoon to the composition of this letter; for which great purpose, Agnes relinquished her desk to me. But first I went downstairs to see Mr Wickfield and Uriah Heep.

I found Uriah in possession of a new, plaster-smelling office, built out in the garden. He received me in his usual fawning way, and pretended not to have heard of my arrival from Mr Micawber; a pretence I took the liberty of disbelieving. He accompanied me into Mr Wickfield's room, which was the shadow of its former self – having been divested of a variety of conveniences, for the accommodation of the new partner – and stood before the fire, warming his back, and shaving his chin with his bony hand, while Mr Wickfield and I exchanged greetings.

'You stay with us, Trotwood, while you remain in Canterbury?' said Mr Wickfield, not without a glance at Uriah for his approval.

So it was settled and, taking my leave of the firm until dinner, I went upstairs again.

I had hoped to have no other companion than Agnes. But Mrs Heep had asked permission to bring herself and her knitting near the fire, in that room. I made a virtue of necessity, and gave her a friendly salutation.

'I'm umbly thankful to you, sir,' said Mrs Heep, in acknowledgement of my inquiries concerning her health, 'but I'm only pretty well. I haven't much to boast of. If I could see my Uriah well settled in life, I couldn't expect much more, I think.'

With a prodigious sniff, she resumed her knitting.

She never left off, or left us for a moment. I had arrived early in the day, and we had still three or four hours before dinner; but she sat there, plying her knitting-needles as monotonously as an hour-glass might have poured out its sands.

What the knitting was, I don't know, but it looked like a net; and as she worked away with those Chinese chopsticks of knitting-needles, she showed in the firelight like an ill-looking enchantress.

At dinner she maintained her watch, with the same unwinking eyes. After dinner, her son took his turn; and when Mr Wickfield, himself, and I were left alone together, leered at me, and writhed until I could hardly bear it. In the drawing-room, there was the mother knitting and watching again. All the time that Agnes sang and played, the mother sat at the piano.

This lasted until bedtime. To have seen the mother and son, like two great bats hanging over the whole house, and darkening it with their ugly forms, made me so uncomfortable, that I would rather have remained downstairs, knitting and all, than gone to bed. I hardly got any sleep. Next day the knitting and watching began again, and lasted all day.

I had not an opportunity of speaking to Agnes, for ten minutes. I could barely show her my letter. I proposed to her to walk out with me; but Mrs Heep repeatedly complaining that she was worse, Agnes charitably remained within, to bear her company. Towards the twilight I went out by myself.

I had not walked out far enough to be quite clear of the town, when I was hailed through the dust, by somebody behind me. The shambling figure, and the scanty great-coat, were not to be mistaken. I stopped, and Uriah Heep came up.

'How fast you walk!' he said. 'My legs are pretty long, but you've given 'm quite a job.'

'Where are you going?' I said.

'I am going with you, Master Copperfield, if you'll allow me the pleasure of a walk with an old acquaintance.'

Saying this, he fell into step beside me.

'To tell you the truth,' I said, 'I came out to walk alone, because I have had so much company.'

He looked at me sideways, and said with his hardest grin: 'You mean mother.'

'Why yes, I do.'

'Ah! But you know we're so very umble,' he returned, 'we must really take care that we're not pushed to the wall by them as isn't umble. All stratagems are fair in love, sir.'

He softly chuckled; looking as like a malevolent baboon, I thought, as any human could look.

'You see,' he said, hugging himself in an unpleasant way, 'you're quite a dangerous rival, Master Copperfield. You always was, you know.'

'Do you suppose,' I said, 'that I regard Miss Wickfield otherwise than as a very dear sister?'

'Well, Master Copperfield,' he replied, 'you may not, you know. But then, you see, you may!'

Anything to equal the low cunning of his visage, and of his shadowless eyes without the ghost of an eyelash, I never saw.

'Come then!' I said. 'For the sake of Miss Wickfield I will tell you what I should, under any other circumstances, as soon have thought of telling to . . . the public hangman. I am engaged to another young lady. I hope that contents you.'

He caught hold of my hand, and gave it a squeeze.

'Oh, Master Copperfield! I'll take off mother directly, and only too appy. I know you'll excuse the precautions of affection, won't you?'

'Before we leave the subject,' I said, 'you ought to understand that I believe Agnes Wickfield to be as far above *you*, and as far removed from all *your* aspirations, as that moon herself!'

'Peaceful, ain't she!' said Uriah. 'Now confess, Master Copperfield, that you haven't liked me all along. You've thought me too umble now, I shouldn't wonder?'

'I am not fond of professions of humility,' I returned.

'There now!' said Uriah. 'Didn't I know it! But how little you think of the rightful umbleness of a person in my station, Master Copperfield! Father and me was both brought up at a foundation school for boys. They taught us all a deal of umbleness – not much else that I know of, from morning to night. We was to know our place, and abase ourselves before our betters. And we had such a lot of betters! Father got made a sexton by being umble. He had the character, among the gentlefolks, of being such a well-behaved man, that they were determined to bring him in. "Be umble, Uriah," says Father to me, "and you'll get on. People like to be above you," says Father, "keep yourself down." I am very umble to the present moment, Master Copperfield, but I've got a little power!'

And he said all this – I knew, as I saw his face in the moonlight – that I might understand he was resolved to recompense himself by using his power.

Whether his spirits were elevated by the communication I had made to him, or by his having indulged in this retrospect, I don't know; but he talked more at dinner than was usual with him.

When we three males were left alone after dinner, he got into a more adventurous state.

'We seldom see our present visitor, sir,' he said, addressing Mr Wickfield, 'and I should propose to give him welcome in another glass or two of wine, if you have no objections. Mr Copperfield, your elth and appiness.'

I pass over Mr Wickfield's proposing my aunt, his proposing Mr Dick, his proposing Doctor's Commons, his proposing Uriah, the struggle between his shame in Uriah's deportment, and his desire to conciliate him.

'Come, fellow-partner!' said Uriah, at last. 'I'll give you another one, and I umbly ask for bumpers, seeing I intend to make it the divinest of her sex.'

Her father had his empty glass in his hand. I saw him set it down, put his hand to his forehead, and shrink back in his elbow-chair.

'Agnes,' said Uriah, 'is, I am safe to say, the divinest of her sex. May I speak out, among friends? To be her father is a proud distinction, but to be her usband . . .'

Spare me from ever again hearing such a cry as that with which her father rose from the table!

'What's the matter?' said Uriah, turning a deadly colour. 'You are not gone mad, after all, Mr Wickfield, I hope? If I say I've an ambition to make your Agnes my Agnes, I have as good a right to it as another man. I have a better right to it than any other man!'

I had my arms round Mr Wickfield, imploring him by everything that I could think of, to calm himself a little. He was mad for the moment; tearing out his hair, beating his head, trying to force me from him, but by degrees he struggled less. At length he said:

'Look at him!'

He pointed to Uriah, pale and glowering in a corner, evidently very much out in his calculations, and taken by surprise.

'Look at my torturer. Before him I have step by step abandoned name and reputation, peace and quiet, house and home. You see the millstone that he is about my neck. You find him in my house, you find him in my business. You heard him, but a little time ago. What need have I to say more?'

The door opened and Agnes, gliding in without a vestige of colour in her face, put her arm round his neck.

'Papa, you are not well. Come with me!'

He laid his head upon her shoulder, as if he were oppressed with heavy shame, and went out with her. Her eyes met mine for but an instant, yet I saw how much she knew of what had passed.

It was dark in the morning, when I got upon the coach at the inn door. The day was just breaking when, struggling up the coach side, came Uriah's head.

'Copperfield!' he said, as he hung by the iron on the roof. 'I thought you'd be glad to hear before you went off, that we've made it all smooth. Though I'm umble, I'm useful to him, you know; and he understands his interest when he isn't in liquor!'

I said I was glad he had made his apology.

'Oh, to be sure!' said Uriah. 'When a person's umble, you know, what's an apology? So easy! I say! I suppose,' with a jerk, 'you have sometimes plucked a pear before it was ripe, Master Copperfield?'

'I suppose I have.'

'*I* did that last night,' said Uriah; 'but it'll ripen yet! It only wants attending to. I can wait!'

37

We had a very serious conversation in Buckingham Street that night about these occurrences. My aunt was deeply interested in them, and walked up and down the room with her arms folded.

I sat down to write my letter to the two old ladies. She read my letter in the morning and approved of it. I posted it, and had nothing to do then but wait, as patiently as I could, for the reply.

At last, an answer came. The Misses Spenlow presented their compliments to Mr Copperfield, and informed him that they had given his letter their best consideration. They added that if Mr Copperfield would do them the favour to call, upon a certain day (accompanied, if he thought proper, by a confidential friend), they would be happy to hold some conversation on the subject.

To this favour, Mr Copperfield immediately replied, with his respectful compliments, that he would have the honour of waiting on the Misses Spenlow, at the time appointed; accompanied, in accordance with their kind permission, by his friend Mr Thomas Traddles of the Inner Temple. Having despatched which missive, Mr Copperfield fell into a condition of strong nervous agitation; and so remained until the day arrived.

It was a great augmentation of my uneasiness to be bereaved, at this eventful crisis, of the inestimable services of Miss Mills. But Mr Mills had taken it into his head that he would go to India, and Julia with him; and Julia went into the country to take leave of her relations.

On our approach to the house where the Misses Spenlow lived, I was at such a discount in respect of my presence of mind, that Traddles proposed a gentle stimulant in the form of a glass of ale. This having been administered at a neighbouring public-house, he conducted me, with tottering steps, to the Misses Spenlow's door.

I had a vague sensation of bowing in great confusion to two dry little elderly ladies, dressed in black.

'Pray,' said one of the two little ladies, 'be seated.'

She appeared to be the manager of the conference, inasmuch as she had my letter in her hand.

'Mr Copperfield!' said the sister with the letter.

I did something – bowed, I suppose – and was all attention, when the other sister struck in.

'My sister Lavinia will state what we consider most calculated to promote the happiness of both parties.'

'Our niece's position,' said Miss Lavinia, 'is much changed by our brother Francis's death. We have no reason to doubt,

Mr Copperfield, that you are a young gentleman possessed of good qualities and honourable character; or that you have an affection for our niece.'

I replied, as I usually did whenever I had a chance, that nobody had ever loved anybody else as I loved Dora. Traddles came to my assistance with a confirmatory murmur.

Miss Lavinia again referred to my letter through her eye-glass.

'You ask permission of my sister Clarissa and myself, Mr Copperfield, to visit here, as the accepted suitor of our niece. Now we have no doubt that you think you like her very much.'

'Think, ma'am,' I began, 'oh! –'

But Miss Clarissa giving me a look (just like a sharp canary), as requesting that I would not interrupt the oracle, I begged pardon.

Miss Lavinia turned my letter and referred through her eye-glass to some orderly-looking notes she had made.

'It seems to us prudent, Mr Traddles, to bring these feelings to the test of our own observation. Therefore, we are inclined so far to accede to Mr Copperfield's proposal, as to admit his visits here.'

'I shall never, dear ladies,' I exclaimed, 'forget your kindness!'

'But,' pursued Miss Lavinia, 'but, we would prefer to regard those visits, Mr Traddles, as made, at present, to us. We must guard ourselves from recognizing any positive engagement between Mr Copperfield and our niece, until we have had an opportunity of observing them.'

'Copperfield,' said Traddles, turning to me, 'you feel, I am sure, that nothing could be more reasonable or considerate.'

'Nothing!' I cried.

'Admitting his visits on this understanding only,' said Miss Lavinia, again referring to her notes, 'we must require from Mr Copperfield a distinct assurance, on his word of honour, that no communication of any kind shall take place between him and our niece without our knowledge.'

I bound myself to the prescribed conditions.

'Sister Clarissa,' said Miss Lavinia, 'the rest is with you.'

Miss Clarissa took the notes and glanced at them.

'We shall be happy,' said Miss Clarissa, 'to see Mr Copperfield to dinner, every Sunday, if it should suit his convenience. Our hour is three.'

I bowed.

'In the course of the week,' said Miss Clarissa, 'we shall be happy to see Mr Copperfield to tea. Our hour is half-past six.'

I bowed again. 'Twice in a week,' said Miss Clarissa, 'but as a rule, not oftener.' I bowed again.

'Miss Trotwood,' said Miss Clarissa, 'mentioned in Mr Copperfield's letter, will perhaps call upon us.'

I intimated that my aunt would be proud and delighted to make their acquaintance; though I must say I was not quite sure of their getting on very satisfactorily together.

Miss Lavinia then arose, and begging Mr Traddles to excuse us for a minute, requested me to follow her. I obeyed, all in a tremble, and was conducted into another room. There, I found my blessed darling stopping her ears behind the door, with her dear little face against the wall; and Jip in the plate-warmer with his head tied up in a towel to stop him barking.

Oh! how beautiful she was in her black frock, and how she sobbed and cried at first, and wouldn't come out from behind the door! How fond we were of one another when she did come out at last; and what a state of bliss I was in, when we took Jip out of the plate-warmer, and restored him to the light, sneezing very much, and were all three reunited!

I had my hands more full than ever, now. My daily journeys to Highgate considered, Putney was a long way off; and I naturally wanted to go there as often as I could.

I was wonderfully relieved to find that my aunt and Dora's aunts rubbed on, all things considered, much more smoothly than I could have expected. My aunt made her promised visit within a few days of the conference; and within a few more days, Dora's aunts called upon her, in due state and form. Similar but more friendly exchanges took place afterwards, usually at intervals of three or four weeks.

38

Weeks, months, seasons, pass along. They seem little more than a summer day and a winter evening. Now, the Common where I walk with Dora is all in bloom, a field of bright gold; and now the unseen heather lies in mounds and bunches underneath a covering of snow. In a breath, the river that flows through our Sunday walks is sparkling in the summer sun, is ruffled by the winter wind, or thickened with drifting heaps of ice.

Not a thread changes in the house of the two little bird-like ladies. The clock ticks over the fireplace, the weather-glass hangs in the hall. Neither clock nor weather-glass is ever right; but we believe in both, devoutly.

I have come legally to man's estate. I have attained the dignity of twenty-one.

Let me think what I have achieved.

I have tamed that savage stenographic mystery. I make a respectable income by it. I am in high repute for my accomplishment in all pertaining to the art, and am joined with eleven others in reporting the debates in Parliament for a morning newspaper.

I have come out in another way. I have taken with fear and trembling to authorship. I wrote a little something, in secret, and sent it to a magazine, and it was published in the magazine. Since then, I have taken heart to write a good many trifling pieces. Now, I am regularly paid for them. Altogether, I am well off.

We have removed from Buckingham Street, to a pleasant little cottage. My aunt, however (who has sold the house at Dover, to good advantage), is not going to remain here, but intends removing herself to a still more tiny cottage close at hand. What does this portend? My marriage? Yes!

Yes! I am going to be married to Dora! Miss Lavinia and Miss Clarissa have given their consent; and if ever canary birds were in a flutter, they are.

Miss Clarissa and my aunt roam all over London, to find out articles of furniture for Dora and me to look at.

Peggotty comes up to make herself useful, and falls to work immediately. Her department appears to be to clean everything over and over again. She rubs everything that can be rubbed, until it shines, like her own honest forehead, with perpetual friction. And now it is that I begin to see her solitary brother passing through the dark streets at night, and looking, as he goes, among the wandering faces. I never speak to him at such an hour. I know too well, as his grave figure passes onwards, what he seeks, and what he dreads.

I am in a dream, a flustered, happy, hurried dream. I can't believe that it is going to be; and yet I can't believe but that everyone I pass in the street, must have some kind of perception that I am to be married the day after to-morrow.

Sophy, Traddles's fiancée, who is to be a bridesmaid in conjunction with Agnes, arrives at the house of Dora's aunts in due course. Traddles presents her to us with great pride.

I have brought Agnes from the Canterbury coach, and her cheerful and beautiful face is among us.

Still I don't believe it. We have a delightful evening, and are supremely happy; but I don't believe it yet. I can't collect myself. I can't check off my happiness as it takes place.

Next day, too, when we all go in a flock to see the house – our house – Dora's and mine – I am quite unable to regard myself as its master. I seem to be there, by permission of somebody else.

Another happy evening, quite as unreal as all the rest of it, and I go home, more incredulous than ever, to a lodging that I have hard by; and get up very early in the morning, to ride to the Highgate Road and fetch my aunt.

I have never seen my aunt in such state. She is dressed in lavender-coloured silk, and has a white bonnet on, and is amazing. Peggotty is ready to go to church, intending to behold the ceremony from the gallery. Mr Dick, who is to give my darling to me at the altar, has had his hair curled. Traddles presents a dazzling combination of cream colour and light blue.

The rest is all a more or less incoherent dream.

A dream of their coming in with Dora; of the clergyman and clerk appearing; of Miss Lavinia being the first to cry; of little Dora trembling very much, and making her responses in faint whispers.

Of my walking so proudly and lovingly down the aisle with my sweet wife upon my arm, through a mist of half-seen people.

Of there being a breakfast, with abundance of things, pretty and substantial, to eat and drink.

Of the pair of hired post-horses being ready, and of Dora's going away to change her dress.

We drive away together, and I awake from the dream. I believe it at last. It is my dear, dear, little wife beside me, whom I love so well!

39

It was a strange condition of things, the honeymoon being over, when I found myself sitting down in my own small house with Dora.

Sometimes of an evening, when I looked up from my writing, and saw her seated opposite, I would lean back in my chair, and think how queer it was that there we were, alone together as a matter of course – nobody's business any more – all the romance of our engagement put away upon a shelf, to rust – no one to please but one another, for life.

When there was a debate, and I was kept out very late, it seemed so strange to me, as I was walking home, to think that Dora was at home!

I doubt whether two young birds could have known less about keeping house, than I and my pretty Dora did. We had a servant, of course. I have still a latent belief that she must have been Mrs Crupp's daughter in disguise, we had such an awful time of it with Mary Anne.

Her name was Paragon. Her nature was represented to us, when we engaged her, as being feebly expressed in her name. She had a written character, as large as a proclamation; and, according to this document, could do everything of a domestic nature that ever I heard of, and a great many things that I never did hear of.

She preyed upon our minds dreadfully. We felt our inexperience, and were unable to help ourselves. We should have been at her mercy, if she had had any; but she was a remorseless woman, and had none.

'My dearest wife,' I said one day to Dora, 'do you think Mary Anne has any idea of time?'

'Why, Doady?' inquired Dora, looking up, innocently, from her drawing.

'My love, because it's five, and we were to have dined at four.'

My little wife came and sat upon my knee, to coax me to be quiet, and drew a line with her pencil down the middle of my nose, but I couldn't dine off that, though it was very agreeable.

'Don't you think, my dear,' I said, 'it would be better for you to remonstrate with Mary Anne?'

'Oh no, please! I couldn't, Doady!' said Dora.

'Why not, my love?'

'Oh, because I am such a little goose,' said Dora, 'and she knows I am!'

I thought this sentiment so incompatible with the establishment of any system of check on Mary Anne, that I frowned a little.

'Oh, what ugly wrinkles in my bad boy's forehead!' said Dora, and still being on my knee, she traced them with her pencil; putting it to her rosy lips to make it mark blacker, and working at my forehead with a quaint little mockery of being industrious, that quite delighted me in spite of myself.

'My precious wife,' I said. 'Come! Sit down on this chair, close beside me! Give me the pencil! There! Now let us talk sensibly. My love, how you tremble!'

'Because I KNOW you're going to scold me!' exclaimed Dora.

'My sweet, I am only going to reason.'

'Oh, but reasoning is worse than scolding!' exclaimed Dora, in despair. 'I didn't marry to be reasoned with. You must be sorry that you married me, or else you wouldn't reason with me!' and she wept most grievously.

I had wounded Dora's soft little heart, and she was not to be comforted. I was obliged to hurry away; I was kept out late; and all night was haunted by a vague sense of enormous wickedness.

It was two or three hours past midnight when I got home. I found my aunt, in our house, sitting up for me.

'Is anything the matter, aunt?' I said, alarmed.

'Nothing, Trot,' she replied. 'Sit down, sit down. Little Blossom has been rather out of spirits, and I have been keeping her company. That's all.'

I leaned my head upon my hand and felt more sorry and

downcast, as I sat looking at the fire, than I could have supposed possible.

'You must have patience, Trot,' said my aunt. 'Rome was not built in a day, nor in a year. You have chosen freely for yourself'; a cloud passed over her face for a moment, I thought; 'and you have chosen a very pretty and a very affectionate creature. It will be your duty, and it will be your pleasure too, to estimate her by the qualities she has, and not by the qualities she may not have. This is marriage, Trot; and Heaven bless you both in it, for a pair of babes in the wood as you are!'

One day my wife planted her chair close to mine, and sat down by my side.

'Will you call me a name I want you to call me?'

'What is it?' I asked with a smile.

'It's a stupid name,' she said, shaking her curls for a moment. 'Child-wife.'

I laughingly asked my child-wife what her fancy was in desiring to be so called. She answered without moving:

'When you are going to be angry with me, say to yourself, "It's only my child-wife!" When I am very disappointing, say, "I knew a long time ago, that she would make but a child-wife!" When you miss what I should like to be, and I think can never be, say, "still my foolish child-wife loves me!" For indeed I do.'

I had a great deal of work to do, and had many anxieties, but I kept them to myself. I am far from sure, now, that it was right to do this, but I did it for my child-wife's sake. I did feel, sometimes, for a little while, that I could have wished my wife had been my counsellor; had had more character and purpose, to sustain me and improve me by; but I felt as if this were an unearthly consummation of my happiness that never had been meant to be.

Thus it was that I took upon myself the toils and cares of our life, and had no partner in them. We lived much as before, in reference to our scrambling household arrangements; but I had got used to those, and Dora I was pleased to see was seldom vexed now. She was bright and cheerful in the old childish way, loved me dearly, and was happy with her old trifles.

40

I must have been married about a year or so, when one evening, as I was returning from a solitary walk, thinking of the book I was then writing, I came past Mrs Steerforth's house. I had often passed it before, but I had never done more than glance at the house, as I went by with a quickened step.

On this occasion, as I walked on, a voice at my side made me start. I was not long in recollecting Mrs Steerforth's little parlour-maid.

'If you please, sir, would you have the goodness to walk in, and speak to Miss Dartle? Miss Dartle saw you pass a night or two ago; and I was to sit at work on the staircase, and when I saw you pass again, to ask you to step in and speak to her.'

I turned back, and was directed to Miss Dartle in the garden. She was sitting on a seat at one end of a kind of terrace.

She saw me as I advanced, and rose to receive me.

'I am told you wish to speak to me, Miss Dartle,' I said,

standing near her, declining her gesture of invitation to sit down.

'If you please,' she said. 'Pray has this girl been found?'

'No.'

'The friends of this excellent and much-injured young lady are friends of yours. Do you wish to know what is known of her?'

'Yes,' I said.

She rose, and taking a few steps towards a wall of holly, said, in a louder voice, 'Come here!' – as if she were calling to some unclean beast. She returned, followed by the respectable Mr Littimer, who, with undiminished respectability, made me a bow, and took up his position behind her.

'Now,' she said, without glancing at him, and touching the old wound as it throbbed; perhaps, in this instance, with pleasure rather than pain. 'Tell Mr Copperfield about the flight.'

'Mr James and myself have been abroad with the young woman, ever since she left Yarmouth under Mr James's protection. We have been in a variety of places, and seen a deal of foreign country. We have been in France, Switzerland, Italy. She was much admired wherever we went.'

Miss Dartle put her hand upon her side. I saw him steal a glance at her, and slightly smile to himself.

'Then I think the young woman began to weary Mr James by giving way to her low spirits and tempers of that kind;

and things were not so comfortable. Mr James he began to be restless again. At last, when there had been, upon the whole, a good many words and reproaches, Mr James he set off one morning from the neighbourhood of Naples, where we had a villa, under pretence of coming back in a day or so, and left it in charge with me to break it that, for the general happiness of all concerned, he was . . . gone. But Mr James, I must say, certainly did behave extremely honourable; for he proposed that the young woman should marry a very respectable person, who was fully prepared to overlook the past, and who was at least as good as anybody the young woman could have aspired to in a regular way: her connexions being very common.'

I was convinced that the scoundrel spoke of himself, and I saw my conviction reflected in Miss Dartle's face.

'The young woman's violence when she came to, after I broke the fact of his departure, was beyond all expectations. She was quite mad, and had to be held by force; or, if she couldn't have got to a knife, or got to the sea, she'd have beaten her head against the marble floor.'

Miss Dartle leaned back upon the seat, with a light exultation in her face.

'It was necessary to take away everything that she could do herself an injury with, or to shut her up close. Notwithstanding which, she got out in the night and never has been seen or heard of, to my knowledge, since.

'I went to Mr James, and informed him of what had

occurred. Words passed between us in consequence, and I felt it due to my character to leave him. I took the liberty of coming home to England, and relating . . .'

'For money which I paid him,' said Miss Dartle.

'Just so, ma'am – and relating what I knew.'

With that, he made a polite bow; and went away through the arch in the wall of holly by which he had come.

Reflecting on what had been thus told me, I felt it right that it should be communicated to Mr Peggotty. On the following evening, I went into London to the lodging he kept, over the little chandler's shop in Hungerford Market. He was sitting reading by a window in which he kept a few plants.

'Mr Peggotty,' I said, taking the chair he handed me, 'don't expect much! I have heard some news.'

He sat down, looking intently at me, and listened in profound silence to all I had to tell. When I had done, he shaded his face, and continued silent. Then he put his hand down firmly on the table.

'My niece, Em'ly, is alive, sir!' he said.

'If she should come here,' I said, 'I believe there is one person more likely to discover her than any other in the world. Do you remember her great friend Martha?'

'I have seen her in the streets,' he said.

'Do you think that you could find her?'

'I think, Mas'r Davy, I know wheer to look.'

'Shall we try to find her tonight?'

He assented, and prepared to accompany me.

'The time was, Mas'r Davy,' he said, as we came downstairs, 'when I thowt this girl, Martha, a'most like the dirt underneath my Em'ly's feet. God forgive me, theer's a difference now!'

We went through Temple Bar, into the city. Not far from Blackfriars Bridge, he pointed to a solitary female figure flitting along the opposite side of the street. I knew it, readily, to be the figure that we sought.

41

We followed at a distance, and were in the narrow water-side street by Millbank before we came up with her. She had strayed down to the river's brink, and stood looking at the water.

I said, 'Martha!'

She uttered a terrified scream, and struggled with me.

'Martha,' I said. 'Do you know who this is, who is with me?'

'Yes,' she said, faintly.

'According to our reckoning,' said Mr Peggotty, 'little Em'ly is like, one day, to make her poor solitary course to London. Help us all you can to find her, and may Heaven reward you!'

She looked at him as if she were doubtful of what he had said.

'Will you trust me?' she asked.

'Full and free!' said Mr Peggotty.

'To speak to her, if I should ever find her; shelter her, if I have any shelter to divide with her; and then bring you to her?'

We both replied together, 'Yes!'

She lifted up her eyes, and solemnly declared that she would devote herself to this task, fervently and faithfully.

We judged it expedient, now, to tell her all we knew; which I recounted at length. She listened with great attention, and asked, when all was told, where we were to be communicated with, if occasion should arise. Under a dull lamp in the road, I wrote our two addresses on a leaf of my pocket-book, which I tore out and gave to her. I asked her where she lived herself. She said, after a pause, in no place long. It were better not to know.

It was midnight when I arrived at home. I had reached my own gate, when I was rather surprised to see that the door of my aunt's cottage was open, and that a faint light in the entry was shining out across the road.

I went to speak to her. It was with very great surprise that I saw a man standing in her little garden. He had a glass and bottle in his hand, and was in the act of drinking. I stopped short, for I recognized the man whom I had once encountered with my aunt in the streets of the city.

The light in the passage was obscured for a moment, and my aunt came out. She was agitated, and told some money into his hand. I heard it chink.

'What's the use of this?' he demanded.

'I can spare no more,' said my aunt. 'You know I have had losses and am poorer than I used to be.'

'Well! I must do the best I can, for the present, I suppose.'

He came slouching out of the garden. Taking two or three quick steps, as if I had just come up, I met him at the gate, and went in as he came out. We eyed one another narrowly in passing, and with no favour.

'Aunt,' I said. 'This man alarming you again! Let me speak to him. Who is he?'

'Child,' returned my aunt, taking my arm, 'come in.'

We sat down in her little parlour.

'Trot,' said my aunt, calmly, 'it's my husband.'

'Your husband, aunt? I thought he was dead!'

'Dead to me,' returned my aunt, 'but living.'

I sat in silent amazement.

'Betsey Trotwood don't look a likely subject for the tender passion,' said my aunt, 'but the time was, Trot, when she believed in that man most entirely. He became an adventurer, a gambler, and a cheat. What he is now, you see.'

My aunt dismissed the matter with a heavy sigh, and smoothed her dress.

'There, my dear!' she said. 'Now you know all about it and we'll keep it to ourselves, Trot!'

42

I had been married, I suppose, about a year and a half. After several varieties of experiment, we had given up the housekeeping as a bad job. The house kept itself, and we kept a page. The principal function of this retainer was to quarrel with the cook.

But, as that year wore on, Dora was not strong. I had hoped that lighter hands than mine would help to mould her character, and that a baby-smile upon her breast might change my child-wife to a woman. It was not to be. The spirit fluttered for a moment on the threshold of its little prison, and, unconscious of captivity, took wing.

'When I can run about again, as I used to do, aunt,' said Dora, 'I shall make Jip race. He is getting quite slow and lazy.'

'I suspect, my dear,' said my aunt, quietly working by her side, 'he has a worse disorder than that. Age, Dora.'

'Do you think he is old?' said Dora, astonished. 'Little Jip! Oh, poor fellow!'

'I dare say he'll last a long time yet, Blossom,' said my

aunt, patting Dora on the cheek. 'But if you want a dog to race with, little Blossom, he has lived too well for that, and I'll give you one.'

'Thank you, aunt,' said Dora. 'But don't, please! I couldn't care for any other dog but Jip.'

'To be sure!' said my aunt, patting her on the cheek again. 'You are right.'

My pretty Dora! When she came down to dinner on the ensuing Sunday, and was so glad to see old Traddles (who always dined with us on Sunday), we thought she would be 'running about as she used to do', in a few days. But they said, wait a few days more, and then, wait a few days more; and still she neither ran nor walked. She looked very pretty, and was very merry; but the little feet that used to be so nimble when they danced round Jip, were dull and motionless.

I began to carry her downstairs every morning, and upstairs every night. She would clasp me round the neck and laugh the while, as if I did it for a wager. My aunt, the best and most cheerful of nurses, would trudge after us, a moving mass of shawls and pillows. Mr Dick would not have relinquished his post of candle-bearer to anyone alive. Traddles would be often at the bottom of the staircase, looking on, and taking charge of sportive messages from Dora to the dearest girl in the world. We made quite a gay procession of it, and my child-wife was the gayest there.

But, sometimes, when I took her up, and felt that she was lighter in my arms, a dead blank feeling came upon me, as if I were approaching to some frozen region yet unseen.

43

I received one morning by the post, the following letter, dated Canterbury, and addressed to me at Doctor's Commons; which I read with some surprise:

'My dear Sir,
'The distinguished elevation to which your talents
have raised you, deters me from presuming to address
the companion of my youth by the familiar appellation
of Copperfield!

'You will naturally inquire by what object am I
influenced in inditing the present missive? Allow me to
say that it is not an object of a pecuniary nature. I may
be permitted to observe, in passing, that my brightest
visions are for ever dispelled – that my peace is shattered
and my power of enjoyment destroyed. The canker is in
the flower. The cup is bitter to the brim. But I will not
digress.

'Placed in a mental position of peculiar painfulness,
beyond the assuaging reach even of Mrs Micawber's

*influence, it is my intention to revisit some metropolitan
scenes of past enjoyment. Among other heavens, my feet
will naturally tend towards the King's Bench Prison. In
stating that I shall be (D.V.) on the outside of the south
wall of that place of incarceration the day after
to-morrow, at seven in the evening, precisely, my object
in this epistolary communication is accomplished. I do
not feel warranted in soliciting my former friends, Mr
Copperfield and Mr Thomas Traddles, to condescend to
meet me. I confine myself to throwing out the observation, that, at the hour and place I have indicated,
may be found such ruined vestiges as yet*

   'Remain,

    'Of

     'A

      'Fallen Tower,

       'WILKINS MICAWBER.

*'P.S. It may be advisable to superadd to the above, the
statement that Mrs Micawber is* not *in confidential
possession of my intentions.'*

I read the letter over several times. Traddles found me in
the height of my perplexity.

'My dear fellow,' I said, 'I never was better pleased to
see you. I have received a very singular letter from Mr
Micawber.'

'No?' cried Traddles. 'And I have received one from Mrs Micawber!'

With that, Traddles produced his letter and made an exchange with me. I watched him into the heart of Mr Micawber's letter, and I then entered on the perusal of Mrs Micawber's epistle.

'Though harrowing to myself to mention, the alienation of Mr Micawber (formerly so domesticated) from his wife and family, is the cause of my addressing my unhappy appeal to Mr Traddles, and soliciting his best indulgence. Mr T. can form no adequate idea of the change in Mr Micawber's conduct, of his wildness, of his violence. The quick eye of affection is not easily blinded, when of the female sex. Mr Micawber is going to London. The West-End destination of the coach, is the Golden Cross. Dare I fervently implore Mr T. to see my misguided husband, and to reason with him? Dare I ask Mr T. to endeavour to step in between Mr Micawber and his agonized family?

'Mr Thomas Traddles's respectful friend and suppliant,

'EMMA MICAWBER.'

'What do you think of that letter?' said Traddles.

'What do you think of the other?' I said.

'I think that the two together, Copperfield,' replied

Traddles, 'mean more than Mr and Mrs Micawber usually mean in their correspondence – but I don't know what.'

We appeared at the stipulated place a quarter of an hour before the time, and found Mr Micawber already there. When we accosted him, his manner was something more confused, and something less genteel, than of yore.

'Gentlemen!' said Mr Micawber, after the first salutations, 'you are friends in need, and friends indeed. Allow me to offer my inquiries with reference to the physical welfare of Mrs Copperfield *in esse*, and Mrs Traddles *in posse*, – presuming, that is to say, that my friend Mr Traddles is not yet united to the object of his affections.'

We acknowledged his politeness, and made suitable replies.

Turning from the building, Mr Micawber accepted my proffered arm on one side, and the proffered arm of Traddles on the other, and walked away between us.

I mentioned that it would give me great pleasure to introduce him to my aunt, if he would ride out to Highgate, where a bed was at his service.

'Gentlemen,' returned Mr Micawber, 'do with me as you will. I am a straw upon the surface of the deep.'

We went to my aunt's house rather than to mine, because of Dora's not being well. My aunt presented herself on being sent for, and welcomed Mr Micawber with gracious cordiality. Mr Dick was at home. He was by nature so exceedingly compassionate of anyone who seemed to be ill at ease, that he shook hands with Mr Micawber at least half-a-dozen times in five minutes.

'You are a very old friend of my nephew's, Mr Micawber,' said my aunt. 'I wish I had had the pleasure of seeing you before.'

'Madam,' returned Mr Micawber, 'I wish I had had the honour of knowing you at an earlier period. I was not always the wreck you at present behold.'

He pulled out his pocket-handkerchief, and burst into tears.

'Mr Micawber,' I said. 'What is the matter? Pray speak out. You are among friends.'

'What is the matter? Villainy is the matter; baseness is the matter; deception, fraud, conspiracy, are the matter; and the name of the whole atrocious mass is – HEEP!'

My aunt clapped her hands, and we all started up.

'The struggle is over!' said Mr Micawber, violently gesticulating with his pocket-handkerchief, and fairly striking out from time to time with both arms, as if he were swimming under superhuman difficulties. 'I will lead this life no longer. I'll put my hand in no man's hand until I have – blown to fragments – the – a – detestable – serpent – HEEP! I'll partake of no one's hospitality. Refreshment – a – underneath this roof – particularly Punch – would – a – choke me – unless – I had previously – choked the eyes – out of the head – a – of – interminable cheat, and liar – HEEP!'

I really had some fear of Mr Micawber's dying on the

spot. The manner in which he struggled through these inarticulate sentences, and, whenever he found himself getting near the name of Heep, brought it out with a vehemence little less than marvellous, was frightful. When he sank into a chair, steaming, and looked at us, he had the appearance of being in the last extremity. I would have gone to his assistance, but he waived me off, and wouldn't hear a word.

'No, Copperfield! – No communication – a – until – Miss Wickfield – a – redress from wrongs inflicted by consummate scoundrel – HEEP!'

With this last repetition of the magic word, Mr Micawber rushed out of the house. But even then his passion for writing letters was too strong to be resisted; for while we were yet in the height of our excitement, hope, and wonder, a note was brought to me from a neighbouring tavern, in which Mr Micawber earnestly requested all our presences at a certain public house in Canterbury, that day week.

44

By this time, some months had passed since our inter-view on the bank of the river with Martha. I had never seen her since, but she had communicated with Mr Peggotty on several occasions. No clue had been obtained to Emily's fate. I confess that I began to despair of her recovery. His conviction remained unchanged. He never wavered in his solemn certainty of finding her.

I was walking alone in the garden, one evening. There was a little green perspective of trellis-work and ivy at the side of our cottage. I happened to turn my eyes towards the place, and I saw a figure beyond, dressed in a plain cloak. It was bending eagerly towards me, and beckoning.

'Martha!' I said.

'Can you come with me?' she inquired. 'I have been to him, and he is not at home. I wrote down where he was to come, and left it on his table with my own hand. I have tidings for him. Can you come directly?'

My answer was to pass out of the gate immediately. I stopped an empty coach that was coming by, and we got into it. When I asked her where the coachman was to drive, she answered:

'Anywhere near Golden Square! And quick!' – then shrunk into a corner, with one trembling hand before her face.

Now dazzled with conflicting gleams of hope and dread, I looked at her for some explanation. But seeing how strongly she desired to remain quiet, I did not attempt to break the silence.

We alighted at one of the entrances to the Square. She hurried me on to one of the sombre streets, and beckoned me to follow her up a common staircase. We proceeded to the top-storey of the house. As we turned to ascend the last flight of stairs between us and the roof, we caught a full view of a female figure pausing for a moment, at a door. Then it turned the handle, and went in.

'What's this!' said Martha. 'She has gone into my room. I don't know her!'

I knew her. I had recognized her, with amazement, for Miss Dartle.

Martha softly led me up the stairs and then, by a little back door, into a small empty garret with a low sloping roof, little better than a cupboard. Between this and the room she had called hers, there was a small door of communication, standing partly open. Here we stopped, breathless with our ascent, and she placed her hand lightly on my lips. I could not see Miss Dartle, or the person whom we had heard her address.

'It matters little to me her not being at home,' said Rosa Dartle. 'I know nothing of her. It is you I come to see.'

'Me?' replied a soft voice.

It was Emily's!

'Yes,' returned Miss Dartle, 'I have come to look at you. I have come to see James Steerforth's fancy.'

There was a rustle, as if the unhappy girl ran towards the door.

'Stay there!' said Miss Dartle. 'If you try to evade *me*, I'll stop you, if it's by the hair.'

A frightened murmur was the only reply that reached my ears. I did not know what to do. Much as I desired to put an end to the interview, I felt that I had no right to present myself.

'Oh, for Heaven's sake, spare me!' exclaimed Emily. 'Whoever you are, you know my pitiable story, and for Heaven's sake spare me.'

'Reserve your false arts for your dupes. Do you hope to move *me* by your tears? No more than you could charm me by your smiles, you purchased slave. Do you know what you have done? Do you ever think of the home you have laid waste?'

'Oh, is there ever a night or day, when I don't think of it!' cried Emily; and now I could just see her, on her knees, with her head thrown back, her pale face looking upward, her hands wildly clasped and held out, and her hair streaming about her. 'Has there ever been a single minute, waking or sleeping, when it hasn't been before me!'

Rosa Dartle sat looking down upon her, as inflexible as a figure of brass.

'The miserable vanity of these earth-worms! *Your* home! Do you imagine that I suppose you could do any harm to that low place? I speak of *his* home – where I live.'

'If you live in his home and know him,' cried Emily, 'you know, perhaps, what his power with a weak, vain girl might be. I don't defend myself, but I know well, and he knows well, that he used all his power to deceive me, and that I believed him, trusted him, and loved him!'

Rosa Dartle recoiled; and in recoiling struck at her. The blow, which had no aim, fell upon the air.

'*You* love him? *You?*' she cried, with her clenched hand quivering, as if it only wanted a weapon to stab the object of her wrath.

'Attend to what I say. Hide yourself somewhere beyond reach. If you live here to-morrow, I'll have your story and your character proclaimed on the common stair. If, leaving here, you seek any refuge in this town, the same service shall be done you.'

Would he never come? How long was I to bear this? How long could I bear it?

'Oh me, oh me!' exclaimed the wretched Emily, and might have touched the hardest heart, I should have thought; but there was no relenting in Rosa Dartle's smile. 'What shall I do!'

'Do?' returned the other. 'There are doorways and dust-heaps – find one and take your flight to Heaven!'

I heard a distant foot upon the stairs. I knew it, I was certain. It was his, thank God.

She moved slowly before the door when she said this, and passed out of my sight.

The foot upon the stairs came nearer – nearer – passed her as she went down – rushed into the room!

'Uncle!'

A fearful cry followed the word. I paused a moment, and looking in, saw him supporting her insensible figure in his arms. He gazed for a few seconds in the face; then stooped to kiss it.

'Mas'r Davy,' he said, 'I thank my Heav'nly Father as my dream's come true! I thank Him hearty for having guided of me, in His own ways, to my darling!'

45

It was yet early in the morning of the following day, when, as I was walking in my garden with my aunt, Mr Peggotty came into the garden. She walked up with a cordial face, shook hands with him, and patted him on the arm.

Then she drew her arm through Mr Peggotty's, and walked with him to a leafy little summer-house there was at the bottom of the garden, where she sat down on a bench, and I beside her. There was a seat for Mr Peggotty too, but he preferred to stand, leaning his hand on the small rustic table.

'I took my dear child away last night to my lodging, wheer I have a long time been expecting of her and preparing fur her. It was hours afore she knowed me right; and when she did, she kneeled down at my feet, and kinder said to me, as if it were her prayers, how it all come to be.

'All night long we have been together, Em'ly and me; and we knows full well, as we can put our trust in one another, ever more.'

'Have you made up your mind,' I said, 'as to the future, good friend?'

'Quite, Mas'r Davy,' he returned; 'and told Em'ly. Theer's mighty countries, far from heer. Our future life lays over the sea. No one can reproach my darling in Australia. We will begin a new life over theer!'

46

When the time Mr Micawber had appointed, so mysteriously, was within four-and-twenty hours of being come, my aunt and I consulted how we should proceed; for my aunt was very unwilling to leave Dora. Ah! how easily I carried Dora up and down stairs, now!

We were disposed, notwithstanding Mr Micawber's stipulation for my aunt's attendance, to arrange that she should stay at home, when Dora unsettled us. 'Why shouldn't you both go? I am not very ill indeed. Am I?'

'Why, what a question!' cried my aunt.

'Yes! I know I am a silly little thing!' said Dora, slowly looking from one of us to the other, and then putting up her pretty lips to kiss us as she lay upon her couch. 'Well, then, you must both go or I shall not believe you; and then I shall cry!'

We agreed, without any more consultation, that we would both go, and my aunt, Mr Dick, Traddles, and I, went down to Canterbury by the Dover mail that night.

At the hotel where Mr Micawber had requested us to

await him, I found a letter, importing that he would appear in the morning punctually at half-past nine.

We all became very anxious and impatient, when we sat down to breakfast. But at the first chime of the half hour, he appeared in the street.

'Gentlemen and madam,' said Mr Micawber, 'good morning! My dear sir,' to Mr Dick, who shook hands with him violently, 'you are extremely good, Mr Dixon.'

Mr Dixon was so pleased with his new name, and appeared to think it so very obliging in Mr Micawber to confer it upon him, that he shook hands with him again.

'Now, sir,' said my aunt to Mr Micawber, 'we are ready for Mount Vesuvius, or anything else, as soon as *you* please.'

'Madam,' returned Mr Micawber, 'I trust you will shortly witness an eruption. Mr Copperfield, I would beg to be allowed a start of five minutes by the clock, and then to receive the present company, inquiring for Miss Wickfield, at the office of Wickfield and Heep, whose stipendiary I am.'

With which, to my infinite surprise, he included us all in a comprehensive bow, and disappeared.

I took out my watch, and counted off the five minutes. When the time was expired, we all went out together to the old house, without saying one word on the way.

We found Mr Micawber at his desk, either writing, or pretending to write, hard.

As it appeared to me that I was expected to speak, I said: 'How do you do, Mr Micawber?'

'Mr Copperfield?' said Mr Micawber. 'I hope I see you well?'

'Is Miss Wickfield at home?' I said.

'Mr Wickfield is unwell in bed, sir, of a rheumatic fever, but Miss Wickfield, I have no doubt, will be happy to see old friends. Will you walk in, sir?'

He preceded us to the dining-room and, flinging open the door of Mr Wickfield's former office, said:

'Miss Trotwood, Mr David Copperfield, Mr Thomas Traddles, and Mr Dixon!'

I had not seen Uriah Heep for some time. Our visit astonished him, evidently. A moment afterwards, he was as fawning and as humble as ever.

'Well, I am sure,' he said, 'this is indeed an unexpected pleasure! Mr Copperfield, I hope I see you well, and – if I may umbly express myself so – friendly towards them as is ever your friends, whether or not.'

I was prevented from responding by the entrance of Agnes, now ushered in by Mr Micawber. She was not quite so self-possessed as usual, I thought.

I saw Uriah watch her while she greeted us; and in the meanwhile, some slight sign passed between Mr Micawber and Traddles; and Traddles, unobserved except by me, went out.

'Don't wait, Micawber,' said Uriah.

Mr Micawber, with his hand upon the ruler stuck into

his waistcoat, stood erect before the door, most unmistakably contemplating one of his fellow-men.

'If there is a scoundrel on this earth,' said Mr Micawber, 'that scoundrel's name is – HEEP!'

Uriah fell back, as if he had been struck or stung. Looking slowly round upon us, he said:

'Oho! This is a conspiracy! You have met here by appointment! You are playing Booty with my clerk, are you, Copperfield? Now take care. None of your plots against me; I'll counterplot you! Micawber, you be off. I'll talk to you presently.'

'Mrs Heep is here, sir,' said Traddles, returning with that worthy mother of a worthy son. 'I have taken the liberty of making myself known to her.'

'Who are you to make yourself known?' retorted Uriah. 'And what do you want here?'

'I am the agent and friend of Mr Wickfield, sir,' said Traddles, 'and I have a power of attorney from him in my pocket, to act for him in all matters.'

'The old ass has drunk himself into a state of dotage,' said Uriah, turning uglier than before, 'and it has been got from him by fraud!'

'Something has been got from him by fraud, I know,' returned Traddles; 'and so do you. We will refer that question, if you please, to Mr Micawber.'

'Ury –!' Mrs Heep began, with an anxious gesture.

'You hold your tongue, mother,' he returned; 'least said, soonest mended.'

Though I had long known that his civility was false, I had had no adequate conception of the extent of his hypocrisy, until I now saw him with his mask off. The suddenness with which he dropped it, when he perceived that it was useless to him; the malice, insolence, and hatred, he revealed at first took even me by surprise, who had known him so long, and disliked him so heartily.

Mr Micawber, whose impetuosity I had restrained thus far with the greatest difficulty, drew the ruler from his breast (apparently as a defensive weapon), and produced from his pocket a foolscap document, folded in the form of a large letter. Opening this packet, with his old flourish, he began to read as follows:

'"Dear Miss Trotwood and gentlemen –"'

'Bless and save the man!' exclaimed my aunt in a low voice. 'He'd write letters by the ream, if it was a capital offence!'

Mr Micawber, without hearing her, went on.

'"In appearing before you to denounce probably the most consummate Villain that ever existed,"' Mr Micawber, without looking off the letter, pointed the ruler, like a ghostly truncheon, at Uriah Heep, '"I ask no consideration for myself. I have ever been the sport and toy of debasing circumstances."'

Mr Micawber, when he was sufficiently cool, proceeded.

'"The stipendiary emoluments, in consideration of which I entered into the service of HEEP, were not defined, beyond the pittance of twenty-two shillings and six per week. The rest was left contingent on the value of my professional exertions; in other and more expressive words, on the baseness of my nature, the cupidity of my motives, the poverty of my family.

'"Heep began to favour me with just so much of his confidence, as was necessary to the discharge of his infernal business. Then it was that I found that my services were constantly called into requisition for the falsification of business, and the mystification of an individual whom I will designate as Mr W. That Mr W. was imposed upon, kept in ignorance, and deluded, in every possible way. My object, when the contest within myself between stipend and no stipend, baker and no baker, existence and non-existence, ceased, was to take advantage of my opportunities to discover and expose the major malpractices committed, to that gentleman's grievous wrong and injury, by HEEP.

'"My charges against HEEP,"' he read on, glancing at him, and drawing the ruler into a convenient position under his left arm, in case of need, '"are as follows."'

We all held our breath, I think. I am sure Uriah held his.

'"First,"' said Mr Micawber, '"when Mr W.'s faculties and memory for business became weakened and confused, HEEP obtained Mr W.'s signature to documents of importance.

He induced Mr W. to empower him to draw out, thus, one particular sum of trust-money, amounting to twelve six fourteen, two and nine, and employed it to meet pretended business charges which were either already provided for, or had never really existed."'

'You shall prove this, you Copperfield!' said Uriah, with a threatening shake of the head.

'Ask HEEP, Mr Traddles, if he ever kept a pocket-book and believes it burnt. If he says yes, and asks you where the ashes are, refer him to Wilkins Micawber, and he will hear of something not at all to his advantage!'

These words had a powerful effect in alarming the mother; who cried out, 'Ury, Ury! Be umble, and make terms, my dear.'

'Mother!' he retorted. 'Will you keep quiet?'

'"Second. HEEP has, on several occasions, systematically forged, to various entries, books, and documents, the signature of Mr W.; and has distinctly done so in one instance, capable of proof by me. The signatures to this instrument, purporting to be executed by Mr W. and attested by Wilkins Micawber, are forgeries by HEEP. I have, in my possession, in his hand and pocket-book, several similar imitations of Mr W.'s signature, here and there defaced by fire, but legible to anyone. I never attested any such document. And the document itself, which I had in my possession, has since been relinquished to Mr Traddles."'

'It is quite true,' assented Traddles.

'Ury, Ury!' cried the mother. 'Be umble and make terms.

I know my son will be umble, gentlemen, if you'll give him time to think. Mr Copperfield, I'm sure you know that he is always very umble, sir.'

It was singular to see how the mother still held the old trick, when the son had abandoned it as useless.

Mr Micawber resumed his letter.

'"Third. And last. I am now in a condition to show, by HEEP's false books. and HEEP's real memoranda, that Mr W. has been for years deluded and plundered, in every conceivable manner, to the pecuniary aggrandisement of the avaricious, false, and grasping HEEP. That his last act, completed but a few months since, was to induce Mr W. to execute a relinquishment of his share in the partnership, and even a bill of sale on the very furniture of his house, in consideration of a certain annuity, to be paid by HEEP in each and every year. All this I undertake to show. Probably much more!"'

I whispered a few words to Agnes, who was weeping half joyfully, half sorrowfully, at my side.

There was an iron safe in the room. The key was in it. A hasty suspicion seemed to strike Uriah; and, with a glance at Mr Micawber, he went to it, and threw the doors clanking open. It was empty.

'Where are the books?' he cried. 'Some thief has stolen the books!'

Mr Micawber tapped himself with the ruler.

'*I* did.'

'Don't be uneasy,' said Traddles. 'They have come into my possession. I will take care of them, under the authority I mentioned. I will tell you what must be done. First, the deed of relinquishment, that we have heard of, must be given over to me now – here. Then, you must prepare to make restoration to the last farthing. All the partnership books and papers must remain in our possession; all your books and papers; all money, accounts and securities, of both kinds. In short, everything here. And until everything is done to our satisfaction, we shall, in short, compel you to keep to your own room.'

'I won't do it!' said Uriah.

'Maidstone Jail is a safer place of detention,' said Traddles. 'Copperfield, will you go round to the Guildhall, and bring a couple of officers?'

Here Mrs Heep broke out again, crying on her knees to Agnes to interfere in their behalf.

'Mother, hold your noise. Well! Let 'em have that deed,' and without lifting his eyes from the ground, Uriah shuffled across the room with his hand to his chin, and slunk out at the door.

47

I must pause yet once again. I am again with Dora in our cottage. I do not know how long she has been ill. I am so used to it in feeling, that I cannot count the time.

It is evening; I sit by the same bed, with the same face turned towards me. I have ceased to carry my light burden up and down stairs now. She lies here all the day.

'Doady!'

'My dear Dora!'

'You won't think what I am going to say, unreasonable, after what you told me, such a little while ago, of Mr Wickfield's not being well? I want to see Agnes. Very much I want to see her.'

It is night; and I am with her still. Agnes has arrived; has been among us for a whole day and an evening. She, my aunt, and I, have sat with Dora since the morning, all together. We have not talked much, but Dora has been perfectly contented and cheerful. We are now alone.

Do I know, now, that my child-wife will soon leave me? They have told me so; but I am far from sure that I have taken that truth to heart. I hold her hand in mine, I hold her heart in mine, I see her love for me, alive in all its strength. I cannot shut out a pale lingering shadow of belief that she will be spared.

'I am going to speak to you, Doady. I am going to say something I have often thought of saying, lately. You won't mind?' with a gentle look.

'Mind, my darling?'

'Doady, dear, I am afraid I was too young.'

I lay my face upon the pillow by her, and she looks into my eyes, and speaks very softly.

'I am afraid, dear, I was too young. I don't mean in years only, but in experience, and thoughts, and everything. I was such a silly little creature.'

'We have been very happy, my sweet Dora.'

'I was very happy, very. But, as years went on, my dear boy would have wearied of his child-wife. She wouldn't have improved. It is better as it is.'

'Oh, Dora, dearest, dearest, do not speak to me so. Every word seems a reproach!'

'No, not a syllable!' she answers, kissing me. 'Oh, my dear, you never deserved it. Now I want to speak to Agnes. When you go downstairs, tell Agnes so, and send her up to me; and while I speak to her, let no one come – not even aunt. I want to speak to Agnes quite alone.'

Agnes is downstairs, when I go into the parlour; and I give her the message. She disappears, leaving me alone with

Jip. He looks at me, crawls to the door, and whines to go upstairs.

'Not tonight, Jip! Not tonight!'

He comes very slowly back to me, licks my hand, and lifts his dim eyes to my face. Then he lies down at my feet, stretches himself out as if to sleep, and with a plaintive cry, is dead.

'Oh, Agnes! Look, look, here!'

That face, so full of pity, and of grief.

It is over. Darkness comes before my eyes, and for a time all things are blotted out of my remembrance.

48

How it came to be agreed among us that I was to seek the restoration of my peace in change and travel, I do not distinctly know. I was to go abroad. That seemed to have been determined among us from the first.

At the request of Traddles, most affectionate of friends in my trouble, my aunt, Agnes, and I returned to Canterbury. We proceeded straight to Mr Micawber's house; where, and at Mr Wickfield's, my friend had been labouring ever since our explosive meeting with Uriah Heep. After we were seated, Mr Micawber announced his intention of seeking his and his family's fortune across the seas in Australia.

'Our Boat is on the shore,' he announced, 'and our Bark is on the sea. My eldest daughter attends at five every morning in a neighbouring establishment to acquire the process of milking cows. My younger children are instructed to observe, as closely as circumstances will permit, the habits of the pigs and poultry maintained in the poorer parts of this city. I have myself directed some attention, during the past week, to the art of baking.'

'All very right,' said my aunt encouragingly. 'Mrs Micawber has been busy too, no doubt.'

'I have been corresponding at some length with my family,' said Mrs Micawber. 'For it seems to me that the time has come when the past should be buried in oblivion, and my family be on terms with Mr Micawber.'

I said I thought so, too.

'Mr Micawber being on the eve of commencing a new career,' said Mrs Micawber, 'in a country where there is sufficient range for his abilities, I could wish to see a festive entertainment, to be given at my family's expense, where Mr Micawber's health and prosperity might be proposed.'

'My dear,' said Mr Micawber, 'all I would say is that I can go abroad without your family coming forward to favour me with a parting shove of their cold shoulders. At the same time, if they should condescend to reply to your communications, far be it from me to be a barrier to your wishes.'

The matter being thus amicably settled, Mr Micawber gave Mrs Micawber his arm, and said they would leave us to ourselves, which they ceremoniously did.

'My dear Copperfield,' said Traddles when they were gone, 'I must do Mr Micawber the justice to say that, although he would appear not to have worked to any good account for himself, he is untiring when he works for other people. I never saw such a fellow for diving, day and night, among papers – to say nothing of the immense number of letters he has written.'

'Letters!' cried my aunt. 'I believe he dreams in letters!'

'There's Mr Dick, too,' said Traddles, 'has been doing wonders. As soon as he was released from overlooking Uriah Heep, whom he kept in such charge as I never saw exceeded, he began to devote himself to Mr Wickfield. His real usefulness in our investigations has been quite stimulating.'

'Dick is a very remarkable man,' said my aunt, 'and I always said he was. Trot, you know it.'

'Now let me see,' said Traddles, looking among the papers on the table. 'Having counting our funds and reduced the confusion, it is clear that Mr Wickfield might now wind up his business with no deficiency whatever.'

'Thank Heaven!' cried Agnes. 'And now I will take our future on myself.'

'Have you thought how, Agnes?' I said.

'Often! I am not afraid, dear Trotwood. I am certain of success. So many people know me here and think kindly of me. If I rent the dear old house, and keep a school, I shall be useful and happy.'

My heart was too full for speech, and Traddles pretended for a while to be looking among the papers.

'Next, Miss Trotwood,' he said. 'That financial holding of yours. You believed that five thousand pounds, Consols, had been misappropriated by Mr Wickfield?'

'Of course I did,' said my aunt, 'and was therefore easily silenced. Agnes, not a word!'

'And indeed, they were sold – but I needn't say by whom.'

'And you have really extorted the money back from Heep?'

'The fact is,' said Traddles, 'Mr Micawber had so completely hemmed him in that he could not escape. A remarkable circumstance is that I don't think he grasped this sum to gratify his avarice, so much as his hatred. He said to me that he would even have spent as much to injure Copperfield.'

'And what's become of him?' said my aunt.

'I don't know. He left here with his mother by one of the London night coaches.'

'Touching Mr Micawber . . .' said my aunt.

'A difficult affair,' said Traddles. 'Mr Micawber issued a number of I.O.U.s to Uriah Heep in respect of advances of salary. I don't know when they may be proceeded on, but I anticipate that until the time of his departure, Mr Micawber will be constantly arrested.'

'Then he must be constantly set free again,' said my aunt. 'What's the amount altogether?'

'Mr Micawber makes the amount a hundred and three pounds five.'

'Now, what shall we give him, that sum included?' said my aunt. 'Five hundred?'

Upon this, Traddles and I both struck in at once. We both recommended a small sum in money, and the payment of the Uriah claims as they came in. We proposed that the family should have their passage and their outfit and a hundred pounds. To this I added that I should give some explanation of his character and history to Mr Peggotty –

who would be emigrating with little Emily at the same time – and that Mr Peggotty should be quietly entrusted the discretion of advancing another hundred.

We all entered warmly into these views, and this closed the proceedings of the evening.

49

The time drawing on rapidly for the sailing of the emigrant ship, my good old nurse came up to London. I was constantly with her and her brother, and the Micawbers, but Emily I never saw. I therefore wrote to her. I told her that on my last visit to Yarmouth, Ham had said how much he wished he could ask her forgiveness for having pressed his affections on her. If he hadn't made her promise to marry him, she might have confided in him, and he might have saved her.

Next morning I was roused by the silent presence of my aunt by my bedside.

'Trot, my dear,' she said, when I opened my eyes. 'Mr Peggotty is here. Shall he come up?'

I replied yes, and he soon appeared.

'Mas'r Davy,' he said, 'I gave Em'ly your letter, sir, and she writ this heer, and begged of me fur to ask you to read it.'

I opened it and read as follows.

'I have got your message. What can I write to thank you for your good and blessed kindness to me! I have put the words close to my heart. I shall keep them till I die. They are sharp thorns, but they are such comfort. Now, my dear friend, goodbye for ever. All thanks and blessings.'

'I am thinking . . .' I said.

'Yes, Mas'r Davy?'

'I am thinking that I'll go down again to Yarmouth. There's time, and to spare, before the ship sails. My mind is constantly running on Ham in his solitude. To put this letter in his hand at this time will be a kindness to both of them. I'll go down tonight.'

He went round to the coach office, at my request, and took the box-seat for me on the mail.

There had been a wind all day. In the hour after I started it had much increased, and the sky was more overcast. But as the night advanced, it came on to blow harder and harder, until our horses could scarcely face the wind. Sweeping gusts of rain came up before this storm like showers of steel, and at these times we were fain to stop.

When the day broke, it blew harder and harder. I had been in Yarmouth when the seamen said it blew great gusts, but I had never known the like of this. Long before we saw the sea, its spray was on our lips, and showered salt rain upon us.

I put up at the old inn, and went down to look at the sea, staggering along the street, which was strewn with sand and seaweed, and flying sea-foam. Near the beach, I saw half the people of the town, lurking behind buildings, and found bewailing women whose husbands were away in herring or oyster boats.

The tremendous sea and the awful noise confounded me. As the high watery walls came rolling in, they looked as if they would engulf the town; as the receding wave swept back with a hoarse roar, it seemed to scoop out deep caves in the beach.

Not finding Ham, I made my way to the yard where he worked. I learned there that he had gone to Lowestoft and would be back to-morrow morning.

I was very much depressed in spirits, very solitary; I felt an uneasiness in Ham's not being there. I went back to the inn and ordered dinner, but I could not eat, I could not sit still. Something within me, faintly answering to the storm without, tossed up the depths of my memory and made a tumult in them. At length I went to bed, exceedingly weary and heavy, but on my lying down I was broad awake, and for hours I lay there, listening to the wind and water.

I awoke in broad day to someone knocking and calling at my door.

'What is the matter?' I called.

'A wreck! Close by! Make haste, sir, if you want to see her! It's thought she'll go to pieces every moment.'

I wrapped myself up in my clothes as quickly as I could, and ran into the street. Numbers of people were there before me, all running to the beach. In the unspeakable confusion, I looked out to sea for the wreck and saw nothing. A half-dressed boatman, standing next to me, pointed to the left. Then I saw it, close in upon us.

One mast was broken short off, and lay over the side, entangled in a maze of sail and rigging – and all that ruin, as the ship rolled with an inconceivable violence, beat the side as if it would stave it in.

The ship had struck once, the boatman said in my ear, and then lifted in and struck again. As he spoke, there was a great cry of pity from the beach. Four men arose with the wreck out of the deep, clinging to the rigging of the remaining mast – uppermost, an active figure with curling hair.

There was a bell on board, and as the ship rolled and dashed like a desperate creature driven mad, the bell rang. Its sound, the knell of those unhappy men, was borne towards us on the wind. Again we lost her, and again she rose. Two men were gone. The agony on the shore increased. Men groaned and clasped their hands; women shrieked and turned away their faces. Some ran wildly up and down along the beach, crying for help, where no help could be.

I found myself one of these, when I saw Ham come breaking through to the front. Another cry, and looking to the wreck, we saw the cruel sail, with blow on blow, beat off the lower of the two men and fly up in triumph round the figure left alone upon the mast.

He had a singular red cap on, and he was seen by all of us to wave it. His action brought an old remembrance to my mind.

Ham watched the sea until there was a great retiring wave when, with a glance to those who held the rope which was made fast round his body, he dashed in after it. He made for the wreck, lost beneath the rugged foam. The distance was nothing, but the power of the sea and wind made the strife deadly. At length he neared the wreck. He was so near, when a high, green, vast hill-side of water seemed to leap up into the ship with a mighty bound, and the ship was gone.

They hauled him in to my very feet, insensible, dead. I remained near him while every means of restoration were tried, but he had been beaten to death by the great wave, and his generous heart was stilled for ever.

'Sir,' said a fisherman, who had known me when Emily and I were children, 'will you come over yonder?'

He led me to that part of the shore where she and I had looked for shells – that part where some fragments of the old boat, blown down last night, had been scattered. Among the ruins of the home he had wronged, I saw him lying with his head upon his arm, as I had often seen him lie at school.

No need, Steerforth, to have said: 'Think of me at my best!' I had done that ever and could I change now, looking on this sight?

50

Upon a mellow autumn day, about noon, I arrived at Highgate. The house looked just the same. I gave the little parlour-maid my card to carry in, and sat down in the drawing-room. On her return she said that Mrs Steerforth would be glad to see me in her chamber.

In a few moments I stood before her. At her chair, as usual, was Rosa Dartle. From the first moment of her dark eyes resting on me, I saw she knew I was the bearer of evil tidings. The scar sprang into view that instant.

I besought Mrs Steerforth to prepare herself to bear what I had to tell, but I should rather have entreated her to weep, for she sat like a stone figure. When I had ceased speaking, she said:

'Rosa! Come to me.'

She came, but with no sympathy or gentleness. She confronted his mother, and broke into a frightful laugh.

'Now is your pride appeased?' she said. 'Now has he made atonement to you – with his life! Yes, look at me! Look here –' striking the scar, 'at your dead child's handiwork!'

The moan the mother uttered went to my heart.

'In your pampering of his pride and passion, he did this and disfigured me for life. Look at me, and moan and groan for what you made him. I loved him better than you ever loved him. And I attracted him. When he was freshest and truest, he loved me. Yes, he did! Many a time, when you were put off with a slight word, he has taken me to his heart!'

'Miss Dartle,' I said, 'if you can be so obdurate as not to feel for this afflicted mother . . .'

'Who feels for me?' she retorted. 'She has sown this. Let her moan for the harvest she reaps today!'

51

One thing I had to do was to conceal what had occurred from those who were going away, and to dismiss them on their voyage in happy ignorance. I told Traddles of the terrible event, and he came to help me in this last service.

The Micawber family were lodged in a little, dirty, tumble-down public-house, whose protruding wooden rooms overhung the river. My aunt and Agnes were there, busily making some little extra comforts, in the way of dress, for the children. Peggotty was quietly assisting.

'And when does the ship sail, Mr Micawber?' asked my aunt.

'Madam, I am informed that we must positively be on board before seven to-morrow morning. Now, my friend Mr Thomas Traddles has requested the privilege of ordering the ingredients necessary to the composition of a moderate portion of Punch. Under ordinary circumstances . . .'

'For myself,' said my aunt, 'I will drink all happiness and success to you, Mr Micawber, with the utmost pleasure.'

'And I too,' said Agnes, with a smile.

Mr Micawber immediately descended to the bar, and in due time returned with a steaming jug. A moment later, a boy came in to say that Mr Micawber was wanted downstairs.

'I have a presentiment,' said Mrs Micawber, 'that it is a member of my family.'

Mr Micawber withdrew, and was absent some little time. At length, the same boy reappeared and presented me with a note, from which I learned that Mr Micawber had again been arrested. I went down with the boy to pay the money. On his release, Mr Micawber embraced me with the utmost fervour, and made an entry of the transaction in his pocketbook, being very particular, I recollect, about a halfpenny I inadvertently omitted from my statement of the total.

'I still have a presentiment,' said Mrs Micawber, on our return, 'that my family will appear on board, before we finally depart.'

'I drink my love to you all,' said my aunt. 'And every blessing and success attend you.'

Mr Peggotty put down the two children he had been nursing, one on each knee, to join Mr and Mrs Micawber in drinking to all of us in return. Even the children were instructed each to dip a wooden spoon into Mr Micawber's pot, and pledge us in its contents.

In the afternoon of the next day, my old nurse and I went down to Gravesend. We found the ship in the river, surrounded by a crowd of boats, a favourable wind blowing, the signal for sailing at her mast-head. I hired a boat directly, and we put off to her.

Mr Peggotty was waiting for us on deck, and took us down. It was so confined and dark that, at first, I could make out hardly anything. By degrees, my eyes became more accustomed to the gloom. Among the great beams, bolts and ringbolts of the ship, and the emigrant-berths, and chests and bundles and barrels, were crowded groups of people making new friendships, taking leave of one another, talking, laughing, crying, eating and drinking. Every age and occupation appeared to be crammed into the narrow compass of the 'tween decks.

The time came when all visitors were being warned to leave the ship. My nurse was crying on a chest beside me, and Mrs Gummidge, assisted by a younger stooping woman in black, was busily arranging Mr Peggoty's goods.

'Is there any last wured, Mas'r Davy?' he said. 'Afore we parts?'

'One thing,' I said. 'Martha!'

He touched the younger woman on the shoulder, and Martha stood before me.

'Heaven bless you, you good man,' I cried. 'You take her with you!'

The ship was fast clearing of strangers. The time was come. I embraced him, and took my weeping nurse upon my arm, and hurried away. On deck, I took leave of poor Mrs Micawber. She was looking distractedly about for her family, even then; and her last words to me were that she would never desert Mr Micawber.

We went over the side into our boat, and lay at a little distance. It was then calm, radiant sunset, and every taper line and spar was visible against the glow. As the sails rose to the wind, and the ship began to move, there broke from all the boats three resounding cheers, which those on board took up. And then I saw her at her uncle's side! Surrounded by the rosy light, and standing high upon the deck, Emily clinging to him, and he holding her, they solemnly passed away.

52

I went away from England. I left all who were dear to me, and went away. If my grief were selfish, I did not know it to be so. I mourned for my child-wife; I mourned for him who might have won the love and admiration of thousands, as he had won mine long ago. I mourned for the broken heart that found rest in the stormy sea, and for the simple home where I had heard the night wind blowing, when I was a child.

For many months I travelled, and at times I found letters awaiting me from Agnes. I wrote a story and sent it to Traddles, and he arranged for its publication. Tidings of my growing reputation began to reach me from travellers whom I encountered by chance.

I cannot penetrate the mystery of my own heart as to know when I began to think that I might have set its earliest and brightest hopes on Agnes – that in my wayward boyhood, I had thrown away the treasure of her love. I had always felt my weakness, in comparison with her constancy and fortitude, and now I felt it more and more. Whatever

I might have been to her, or she to me, if I had been more worthy of her long ago, I was not now. The time was past. I had let it go by, and had deservedly lost her.

These were the shifting quicksands of my mind until my return home after three years.

53

I landed in London on a wintry autumn morning. It was dark and raining. My aunt had long been re-established at Dover, and Traddles had chambers in Gray's Inn. They expected me home before Christmas, but had no idea of my returning so soon. I had purposely misled them, that I might have the pleasure of taking them by surprise. And yet, I was perverse enough to feel a chill and disappointment in receiving no welcome, and rattling alone and silent through the misty streets.

I made my way to Gray's Inn, and an inscription on the doorpost of Number Two in the Court informed me that Mr Traddles occupied a set of chambers on the top storey. I ascended the staircase and knocked on the outer door. A considerable scuffling within ensued, but nothing else. I knocked again.

A small sharp-looking lad presented himself.

'Is Mr Traddles within?' I said.

'Yes, sir, but he's engaged.'

'I want to see him.'

The sharp-looking lad decided to let me in, and admitted me to a little sitting-room; where I came into the presence of my old friend (somewhat out of breath), seated at a table, and bending over papers.

'Good God!' cried Traddles, looking up. 'It's Copperfield!' and rushed into my arms, where I held him tight.

'All well, my dear Traddles?'

'All well, my dear, dear Copperfield, and nothing but good news! To think that you should have been so nearly coming home, my dear boy, and not at the ceremony!'

'What ceremony?'

'Didn't you get my last letter? I am married.'

'Married!' I cried joyfully.

'Lord bless me, yes,' said Traddles. 'Why, my dear boy, Sophy's behind the window curtain! Look here!'

To my amazement, she came at that same instant, laughing and blushing, from her place of concealment. And a more cheerful, amiable, bright-looking bride, I believe the world never saw. I kissed her as an old acquaintance should, and wished them joy with all my heart.

'Dear me,' said Traddles, 'what a delightful reunion! How happy I am!'

'And so am I,' I said.

'We all are,' said Traddles. 'Even the girls. Dear me, I forgot them!'

'Forgot?'

'Sophy's sisters,' said Traddles. 'They are staying with us.

They have come to have a peep at London. As it wouldn't look quite professional if they were seen by a client, they decamped. My love, will you fetch the girls?'

Sophy tripped away, and we heard her received in the adjoining room with a peal of laughter.

'Our domestic arrangements are,' said Traddles, 'to say the truth, quite unprofessional altogether, my dear Copperfield. Even Sophy's being here is unprofessional. And we have no other place of abode. Sophy's an extraordinary manager! You'll be surprised how those girls are stowed away.'

'Are many of the young ladies with you?' I enquired.

'Five. Three in that room,' said Traddles, pointing. 'Two in that.'

I could not help glancing round in search of the accommodation remaining for Mr and Mrs Traddles.

'Well,' said Traddles, 'we are prepared to rough it. There's a little room in the roof – a capital gipsy sort of place. There's quite a view from it.'

54

The next day I spent on the Dover coach. I burst safe and sound into my aunt's old parlour while she was at tea, and was received by her, and Mr Dick, and dear old Peggotty, who acted as housekeeper, with open arms and tears of joy.

When we were alone, my aunt and I talked far into the night. How the emigrants wrote home cheerfully and hopefully; how Mr Micawber had actually remitted diverse small sums of money; how Mr Dick incessantly occupied himself in copying everything he could lay his hands on, and kept King Charles the First at a respectful distance by that semblance of employment.

'And when, Trot,' said my aunt, 'are you going over to Canterbury?'

'I shall get a horse and ride over to-morrow morning, aunt. I could not have come through Canterbury today without stopping, if I had been coming to anyone but you.'

She was pleased, but answered:

'My old bones would have kept till to-morrow, Trot,' and

patted my hand, as I sat looking thoughtfully into the fire. When I raised my eyes, I found she was steadily observant of me. Perhaps she had followed the current of my mind.

'Has Agnes any . . .?' I was thinking aloud, rather than speaking.

'I suspect she has an attachment, Trot.'

'If it should be so,' I said, 'Agnes will tell me at her own good time.'

I rode away early in the morning, for the scene of my old school days. The staid old house was just as it had been when I first saw it. I was shown up the grave old staircase into the unchanged drawing-room. Her beautiful serene eyes met mine as she came towards me. She stopped and laid her hand upon her bosom. I caught her in my arms.

'Agnes, my dear girl! I have come too suddenly upon you.'

'No, no! I am so rejoiced to see you, Trotwood!'

I folded her to my heart, and for a while we were silent. I could find no utterance for what I felt. With her own sweet tranquillity, she calmed my agitation, led me back to the time of our parting, spoke to me of Emily, of Dora's grave.

'And you, Agnes,' I said by and by. 'Tell me of yourself.'

'What should I tell? Papa is well; the labour in running the school is so pleasant that it is scarcely grateful to call it by that name; our anxieties are set at rest.'

'Is there nothing else, sister?' I said.

I had sought to lead her to what my aunt had hinted at. I saw, however, that she was uneasy, and I let it pass. When dinner was done, Mr Wickfield, Agnes, and I went upstairs, where Agnes and her little charges sang and played. After the children left us, we three sat together talking of bygone days.

As I rode back in the lonely night, the wind going by me like a restless memory, I feared Agnes was not happy. I was not happy, but thus far I had faithfully set the seal upon the past.

55

For a time, until my book should be completed, I took up my abode in my aunt's house at Dover. Occasionally, I went to London to consult with Traddles on some business point. He had managed for me, in my absence, with the soundest of judgement, and my worldly affairs were prospering. My notoriety began to bring me an enormous quantity of letters, and I agreed with Traddles to have my name painted up on his door. There, at intervals, I laboured through bushels of them, like a Home Secretary of State without the salary.

One day, when we were together in chambers, I said:

'Do you remember that old rascal Creakle? I have here a letter from him.'

'From Creakle, the schoolmaster?' said Traddles. 'No!'

'He's not a schoolmaster now, Traddles. He is retired. He is a Middlesex magistrate, and among the persons who, in my rising fame and fortune, discover they were always much attached to me. He writes here that he will be glad to show me in operation the only true system of prison discipline – the only unchallengeable way of making sincere and lasting penitents – which, as you know, is by solitary confinement. What do you say?'

'To the system?' said Traddles, looking grave.

'No. To my accepting the offer, and your going with me.'

'I don't object.'

I wrote accordingly to Mr Creakle that evening.

On the appointed day, Traddles and I repaired to the prison where Mr Creakle was powerful. It was an immense and solid building, erected at a vast expense. I could not help thinking, as we approached the gate, what an uproar there would have been in the country if any deluded man had proposed to spend one half the money it had cost on the erection of an industrial school for the young, or a house of refuge for the deserving old.

Our old schoolmaster received me like a man who had always loved me tenderly, and Traddles in like manner. Our venerable instructor was a great deal older, and not improved in appearance. His face was as fiery as ever; his eyes were as small, and rather deeper set.

Together with some other visitors, we began our inspection in the great kitchen, where every prisoner's dinner was being set out separately, to be handed to him in his cell. I said aside to Traddles that not one man in five of the great bulk of the honest, working community ever dined half so well. But I learned that the system, which involved the perfect isolation of prisoners, required high living.

When we began to visit individuals in their cells, I heard so repeatedly of a certain Number Twenty-Seven, who appeared to be a model prisoner, that I resolved to suspend my judgement of the system until I should see him.

I had to restrain my impatience for some time, on account of Twenty-Seven being reserved for a concluding effect. But at last we came to the door of his cell, and Mr Creakle, looking through a little hole in it, reported to us in a state of the greatest admiration, that he was reading a Hymn Book.

He then directed the door to be opened, and whom should Traddles and I then behold, to our amazement, but Uriah Heep.

He knew us directly, and his recognition caused a general admiration in the party.

'Well, Twenty-Seven,' said Mr Creakle. 'How do you find yourself today?'

'I am very umble, sir!' replied Uriah Heep.

'You are always so, Twenty-Seven,' said Mr Creakle.

Here another gentleman asked: 'Are you quite comfortable?'

'Yes, I thank you, sir,' said Uriah Heep. 'I see my follies now, sir. That's what makes me comfortable. I have committed follies, gentlemen, and I ought to bear the consequences without repining.'

There was a murmur of gratification at Twenty-Seven's celestial state of mind, but both Traddles and I experienced a great relief when he was again locked in.

'Do you know,' I said, as we walked along the passage, 'what felony was Number Twenty-Seven's last "folly"?'

The answer was that it was fraud, forgery and conspiracy on the Bank of England – a deep plot for a large sum. Sentence, transportation for life.

56

At least once a week, and sometimes oftener, I rode over to Canterbury and passed the evening with Agnes. When I read to her what I wrote, when I saw her listening face, moved her to smiles or tears, I thought what a fate might have been mine – but only thought so. I had worked out my own destiny – won what I had impetuously set my heart on. I had no right to murmur, and must bear.

She did not once show me any change in herself. What she always had been to me, she still was.

But as Christmas-time came round, a doubt began to oppress me – whether she perceived the true state of my feelings but was apprehensive of giving me pain. If that were so, my sacrifice was nothing; my plainest obligation to her unfulfilled. If such a barrier were between us, I resolved to break it down.

It was a cold, harsh, winter day.

'Riding today, Trot?' said my aunt, putting her head in at the door.

'Yes. I am going over to Canterbury. Do you know anything more, aunt, of that attachment of Agnes?'

She looked up in my face a little while, before replying:

'I think I do, Trot. I think Agnes is going to be married.'

'God bless her!' I said cheerfully.

'God bless her!' said my aunt. 'And her husband too!'

I echoed it, and rode away. There was greater reason than before to do what I had resolved to do.

I found Agnes alone, and sat beside her on the window-seat. As I looked at her beautiful face, observant of her work, she raised her mild clear eyes, and saw that I was looking at her.

'You are thoughtful today, Trotwood!'

'Shall I tell you what about? I came to tell you.'

She put aside her work and gave me her whole attention.

'Agnes, I have heard – but from other lips than yours, which seems strange – that there is someone upon whom you have bestowed the treasure of your love. Do not shut me out of what concerns your happiness so nearly! Let me be your friend, your brother, in this matter, of all others!'

With an appealing, almost a reproachful, glance, she rose from the window; and hurrying across the room, put her hands before her face, and burst into such tears as smote me to the heart.

'Agnes! Sister! Dearest! What have I done! If you are unhappy, let me share your unhappiness. If you are in need of help, let me try to give it to you.'

She was quiet now. In a little time she turned her pale face towards me.

'I owe it to your pure friendship for me, Trotwood, to tell you, that if I have any secret, it is no new one. It is not what you suppose. I cannot reveal it. It has long been mine, and must remain mine.'

She was going away, but I detained her. New thoughts and hopes were whirling through my mind, and all the colours of my life were changing.

'Dearest Agnes, whom I so respect and honour – whom I so devotedly love! When I came here today, I thought that nothing could have wrested this confession from me. But, Agnes, if I have indeed any hope that I may ever call you something more than Sister . . . Agnes, ever my guide and best support! If you had been more mindful of yourself, and less of me, when we grew up here together, I think my fancy never would have wandered from you.'

Still weeping, but not sadly – joyfully! And clasped in my arms as she had never been, as I thought she never was to be!

'When I loved Dora – fondly, Agnes, as you know – my love would have been incomplete without your sympathy. I had it, and it was perfected. And when I lost her, Agnes, what should I have been without you! I went away loving you; I stayed away loving you; I returned home loving you.'

She laid gentle hands upon my shoulders and looked calmly in my face.

'There is one thing I must say. Do you know, yet, what it is?'

'Tell me, my dear.'

'I have loved you all my life!'

We were married within a fortnight. As we drove away together, Agnes said:

'Dearest husband, I have one more thing to tell you.'

'Let me hear it, love.'

'It grows out of the night when Dora died. She sent you for me.'

'She did.'

'She made a last request to me, and left me a last charge.'

'And it was . . .?'

'That only I would occupy this vacant place.'

And Agnes laid her head upon my breast and wept; and I wept with her, though we were so happy.

57

What I have purposed to record is nearly finished. But there is yet an incident conspicuous in my memory.

I had advanced in fame and fortune, my domestic joy was perfect, I had been married ten happy years. Agnes and I were sitting by the fire, in our house in London, one night in spring, and three of our children were playing in the room, when I was told that a stranger wished to see me.

'Let him come here,' I said.

There appeared a hale, grey-haired old man. I had not yet clearly seen his face when my wife, starting up, cried out that it was Mr Peggotty.

It *was* Mr Peggotty. When our first emotion was over, and he sat down before the fire with our children on his knees, he looked to me as vigorous and robust an old man as ever I had seen.

'A joyful hour indeed, old friend!' I cried.

'Are you alone?' asked Agnes.

'Yes, ma'am,' he said, kissing her hand. 'Quite alone. It's a mort of water fur to come across, and on'y stay a matter of fower weeks. You see, I doen't grow younger, and if I hadn't sailed as 'twas, most like I shouldn't never have done't. And it's allus been on my mind, as I *must* come and see Mas'r Davy and your own sweet blooming self, in your wedded happiness, afore I got to be too old.'

He looked at us, as if he could never feast his eyes on us sufficiently.

'And now tell us everything relating to your fortunes,' I said.

'We've thrived. What with sheep-farming and stock-farming, and one thing and t'other, we've done nowt but prosper. Em'ly might have married well, a mort of time. "But, uncle," she says, "that's gone for ever." She'll go any distance fur to tend a sick person, or do some kindness tow'rds a young girl's wedding. Liked by young and old; sowt out by all that has any trouble. That's Em'ly.'

'And Mr Micawber,' I said. 'What's the latest news of him?'

Mr Peggotty, with a smile, produced a little odd-looking newspaper and pointed to a certain paragraph. I read it aloud:

'*The public dinner to our distinguished fellow-columnist and townsman, Wilkins Micawber, Esquire, Port Middlebay District Magistrate, came off yesterday in the large room of the Hotel, which was crowded to suffocation. Doctor Mell, who presided, in a speech* replete with feeling, proposed: "Our distinguished guest, the ornament of our town". The cheering with which the toast was received defies description.'

Then Mr Peggotty, pointing to another part of the paper, my eyes rested on my own name, and I read thus:

'To DAVID COPPERFIELD, ESQUIRE,
'THE EMINENT AUTHOR.
   'My dear sir: Years have elapsed since I had an opportunity of perusing the lineaments now familiar to a considerable portion of the civilized world. But, my dear sir, though estranged by the force of circumstances from the personal society of the friend and companion of my youth, I have not been unmindful of his soaring flight. Go on, my dear sir! You are not unknown here; you are not unappreciated. Though remote, we are not slow. Go on, my dear sir, in your eagle course! The inhabitants of Port Middlebay may at least aspire to watch it, with delight, with entertainment, with instruction! Among the eyes elevated towards you from this portion of the globe, will ever be found
               'The
                 'Eye
                   'Appertaining to:
                         'WILKINS MICAWBER,
                               'Magistrate.'

58

And now my story ends. I see myself, with Agnes at my side, journeying along the road of life. I see our children and friends around us. What faces are the most distinct?

Here is my aunt, in stronger spectacles, an old woman but upright yet, and a steady walker of six miles at a stretch in winter weather.

Always with her, here comes Peggotty, my good old nurse, likewise in spectacles, accustomed to do needle-work at night very close to the lamp.

Among my boys, this summer holiday time, I see an old man making giant kites, and gazing at them in the air, with a delight for which there are no words.

Who is this bent lady, supporting herself by a stick? She is in a garden, and near her stands a sharp, dark, withered woman, with a white scar on her lip. Let me hear what they say.

'Rosa, I have forgotten this gentleman's name.'

Rosa bends over her.

'Mr Copperfield.'

'I am glad to see you, sir. You have seen my son, sir? Are you reconciled?'

Looking fixedly at me, she puts her hand to her forehead, and suddenly calls out:

'Rosa, come to me. He is dead!'

Working at his chambers in the Temple, I come upon my dear Traddles. We walk away, arm in arm. I am going to have a family dinner with Traddles. It is Sophy's birthday.

Traddles's house is large, but Traddles keeps his papers in the dressing-room, and his boots with his papers. He and Sophy squeeze themselves into upper rooms, reserving the best bedrooms for the girls – for more of the girls are here, and always are here, by some accident or other, than I know how to count. Here, when we go in, is a crowd of them, running down to the door, and handing Traddles about to be kissed, until he is out of breath.

And now, as I close my task, subduing my desire to linger yet, these faces fade away. But one face, shining on me, is above and beyond them. I turn my head, and see it, in its beautiful serenity, beside me. My lamp burns low, and I have written far into the night, but the dear presence bears me company.

Oh, Agnes, Oh my soul, so may thy face be by mine when I close my life indeed.

So may I, when realities are melting from me like the shadows which I now dismiss, still find thee near me, pointing upward.

DAVID COPPERFIELD

With Puffin Classics, the adventure isn't
over when you reach the final page.
Want to discover more about your favourite
characters, their creators and their worlds?
Read on . . .

CONTENTS

NAME: Charles John Huffam Dickens
BORN: 7 February 1812 in Portsmouth, England
DIED: 9 June 1870 in Gad's Hill, Kent, England (but he is
buried in Poets' Corner in Westminster Abbey, London)
NATIONALITY: English
LIVED: mainly in and around London
MARRIED: to Catherine (Kate) Thomson Hogarth, in 1836;
separated 1858
CHILDREN: ten: Charles, Mary, Kate, Walter, Francis, Alfred,
Sydney, Henry, Dora and Edward

What was he like?

Charles Dickens was a very likeable person. He had a lively
sense of humour and a vivid imagination – he loved playing
with children and had many friends. Charles was a man who
was always on the go. He rarely missed a deadline or let his
fans down, and managed to do this without ever becoming
boring.

He was also very caring and, throughout his life, Dickens
demonstrated empathy for his fellow man. In 1865 he was
on board the train involved in the Staplehurst rail crash. The
carriage in which he was travelling was not badly damaged and
he was lucky enough to emerge unscathed, so he immediately
set about tending to the injured and dying. The incident had
a profound and lasting effect on his life and he became a
dedicated social campaigner and an administrator for several
charitable organizations.

Where did he grow up?

Dickens spent his early childhood in Portsmouth and London. He was the second of eight children. His parents were a lively couple, who enjoyed parties and family gatherings, but the cost of entertaining and raising a large family put them in financial difficulties.

When Dickens was twelve, his father was sent to Marshalsea Prison for debt and so Charles was sent out to work in Warren's Blacking Factory, which produced boot polish, in order to support the family. Charles never forgot the hard labour or the appalling conditions. Although he went back to school, it was an experience he would always remember. When he was fifteen he began to work in a lawyer's office, but he knew it wasn't for him. He found the office so boring that he spent his time dropping cherry stones on to the heads of passers-by from the window! By his early twenties, he had found a job as a parliamentary reporter and, using his knowledge of the law, started reporting on court cases. He filled his spare time writing sketches of London life for newspapers and magazines, and in 1837 he shot to fame with the publication of his first novel, *The Pickwick Papers*.

What did he do apart from writing books?

Dickens loved public speaking and he toured widely both at home and abroad, pouring his boundless energy into lecturing on subjects such as the abolition of slavery, as well as giving readings of his own works.

Another of Dickens's passions was the theatre, for which he wrote a number of plays, as well as performing on stage himself.

Where did Charles Dickens get the idea for David Copperfield*?*

By 1850 Charles Dickens's reputation as one of the great Victorian novelists was firmly established. His readers were keen to learn more about him, so he wrote *David Copperfield*, with many of the storylines echoing his own childhood and adult life. (His father was the inspiration for Mr Micawber, imprisoned for bad debt, and one of Dickens' greatest comic characters.) Dickens admitted that *David Copperfield* was his favourite novel. He once wrote, 'I have in my heart of hearts a favourite child. And his name is David Copperfield.'

What did people think of David Copperfield *when it was first published as a novel in 1850?*

David Copperfield was serialized in monthly instalments from 1849, and each month people could read the next chapter in the story. In November 1850 it was published as a complete novel. By then it was already very well known and the book was highly acclaimed by his readers.

What other books did he write?

Starting with *The Pickwick Papers* in 1837, Dickens wrote over twenty novels, including *Oliver Twist* (1838), *Nicholas Nickleby* (1839), *The Old Curiosity Shop* (1841), *Barnaby Rudge* (1841), *Martin Chuzzlewit* (1843), *A Christmas Carol* (1843), *Bleak House* (1853), *Hard Times* (1854), *A Tale of Two Cities* (1859) and *Great Expectations* (1861).

David Copperfield – the hero and narrator of the novel. The story follows David from his troubled childhood to adulthood. David is a sensitive, gentle boy who suffers at the hands of the cruel Murdstones. As a young adult, he is kind, trusting and naive, but eventually he finds true happiness and becomes a successful writer.

Clara Copperfield – David's beautiful young mother. Widowed six months before David is born, she is a very loving and caring mother, but later is pressured into marriage by Edward Murdstone, whose harsh treatment of David destroys her spirit. She dies with her newborn son while David is away at school.

Uriah Heep – a devious scoundrel who works for Mr Wickfield. Uriah plots against Mr Wickfield and tries to marry his daughter, Agnes. Heep's fake humbleness hides his desire for power and control. He ends up in jail for fraud.

James Steerforth – David's selfish upper-class school friend who ingratiates himself into David's life. Steerforth uses his charms to steal Em'ly away and then cold-heartedly abandons her.

Little Em'ly – the orphaned niece of Daniel Peggotty and David's childhood sweetheart. Em'ly was engaged to Ham Peggotty, but in her desire to be a lady she runs off with James

Steerforth. When Steerforth abandons her, she emigrates to Australia with her uncle.

Miss Betsey Trotwood – David's formidable great-aunt. She is a no-nonsense type of woman but has a heart of gold.

Mr Barkis – a horse-and-cart driver who takes David to Salem House boarding school in London. Shy and quiet, Barkiss woes Clara Peggotty and eventually marries her.

Mr Creakle – the cruel and sadistic headmaster of Salem House where David first goes to school.

Mr Dick – a simple-minded fellow who lodges at Betsey Trotwood's, who becomes a friend of David.

Mr Micawber – Mr Micawber houses David when he first moves to London and they become friends. He is big-hearted but always short of money. Mr Micawber uncovers Uriah Heep's plot against Mr Wickfield and eventually emigrates to Australia with his wife and children.

Mr Murdstone – David's brutal stepfather, who drives his mother Clara to illness and early death.

Miss Jane Murdstone – Mr Murdstone's harsh, unfeeling sister who moves in at her brother's request to help with the family.

Mr Spenlow – A pompous lawyer who objects to David's plans to marry his daughter.

Dora Spendlow – Dora is silly and spoilt, and unable to run the household, but David falls for her childlike beauty and marries her. Dora becomes ill and dies when she's still only young.

Mrs Steerforth – James Steerforth's mother who dotes on her son and spoils him.

Peggotty – the housekeeper and David's loyal nurse, who remains faithful to him all through his life. Clara Peggotty is the aunt of Ham and little Em'ly Peggotty.

Daniel Peggotty – Peggotty's kind-hearted brother who takes in his niece, little Em'ly, and searches for her when she goes off with Steerforth.

Rosa Dartle – Mrs Steerforth's companion. Rosa is in love with Steerforth, but he is not interested in her.

Tommy Traddles – David's good-natured school friend who works hard to make a career for himself.

Agnes Wickfield – the devoted daughter of Mr Wickfield, the lawyer. She becomes very close to David and is his true love. She eventually marries him.

Charles Dickens named some of his children after his favourite authors. Among his ten children were Alfred Tennyson Dickens, Henry Fielding Dickens and Edward Bulwer Lytton Dickens. He also gave them all funny nicknames:

- Charles Jr – 'Charley'
- Mary – 'Mamie'
- Kate – 'Lucifer Box'
- Walter – 'Young Skull'
- Francis – 'Chickenstalker'
- Alfred – 'Skittles'
- Sydney – 'The Admiral'
- Henry – 'Mr H'
- Dora sadly died in infancy
- Edward – 'Plorn'

Charles Dickens's own nickname was 'Boz'. Originally a nickname that Dickens gave his younger brother Augustus, it started out as 'Moses', after a character from a novel, then it became 'Boses' and then it was shortened to Boz, which Charles used as a pen-name when he began publishing his popular series 'Sketches by Boz' in 1833.

Dickens was full of odd habits. He touched objects three times for good luck, and the furniture in his house had to be in a certain position before he could concentrate on his work.

He was also obsessed with cleanliness and kept everything very neat and tidy.

He was very particular about his appearance, combing his hair hundreds of times a day and constantly checking himself in the mirror.

Dickens was described by many as a jolly man who loved playing practical jokes on people, especially his close friends. Charles was very good friends with Hans Christian Andersen, who dedicated one of his books to him.

In 1842 Charles and his wife Catherine sailed to North America, landing first in Boston, where Charles was greeted like a Victorian-era pop idol! During their time in America, they made many lifelong friends, including the famous poet Henry Wadsworth Longfellow.

In November 1867, despite being very frail, Dickens sailed back to America for a five-month reading tour. He performed in Boston and New York, Washington DC, Philadelphia, Buffalo, New Haven, Worcester, and Portland, Maine. The tour was a huge success and he earned a massive £20,000 fortune.

David Copperfield is a story of growing up in Victorian England, with a cast of characters designed to show the many social themes that run through the novel, such as poverty and education. These social issues were close to Dickens's heart. What other themes are you able to identify, and which do you think is the most important one in the story?

Think about the plot and your favourite characters. Which part of David's life story did you enjoy the most?

Who are the most memorable characters in the story and why?

Charles Dickens's characters are well known for having memorable, evocative names. How do the characters' names in *David Copperfield* reflect their personalities?

Even though *David Copperfield* was published over 150 years ago, the story is as popular today as it ever was. Why do you think that is?

Happy birthday, Charles! On 7 February 2012 Dickens would have celebrated his 200th birthday! Think of all the changes that have happened in the world since he was alive, and do you think there are any things that haven't changed much at all?

Make a timeline of David's life. Where on the timeline do you think his life changed the most? Perhaps when his mother died or when he ran away from the factory?

Charles Dickens gave all his characters vivid personalities. Draw caricatures of your four favourite characters, remembering to accentuate certain features that are memorable to that person.

David Copperfield is based around Charles Dickens's own life. Could you write a short chapter of your life? What name would you give yourself and what would you consider your most significant moments – perhaps starting school, or a particular holiday?

Many of Charles Dickens's novels were originally published with illustrations. Choose a part of the story and create your own illustrations for it.

Research the Victorian era on the Internet to find out more about what it would have been like to live in Dickens's time.

If you have enjoyed reading *David Copperfield*, try another novel by Charles Dickens, such as *Oliver Twist*, *A Christmas Carol* or *Great Expectations*, all available in Puffin Classics.

affront – to offend or insult, particularly in public

altercation – a heated argument

annuity – money paid each year as an allowance or income.

approbation – praise, approval

avocation – hobby, or usual work

Borough – a name given to the district of Southwark, in London. It lies south of the River Thames, and is opposite the City of London

chay – a light travelling carriage, or chaise. Some people thought the French word 'chaise' was plural, so invented 'chay' as the singular version

Consols – short for Consolidated Annuities. These are government securities: people can invest – put their money into the funds in return for a government bond – and the government pays interest four times a year on the money that has been invested. Consols were first issued in 1751, and are still available

counting-house – an office from which a business does its accounts and correspondence

cupidity – greed for money and riches

deferential – politely respectful

Doctors' Commons – a society of lawyers practising canon (church) and civil law. They had buildings near St Paul's Cathedral where members lived and worked, and where there were also civil law courts. Wills were kept there, and marriage licences granted. As new laws came into force, other groups of lawyers took over work that Doctors' Commons had dealt with. Eventually the buildings were pulled down in 1867

domiciliary accommodation – a place to live

dotage – being silly, too fond of something, feeble-minded: a state usually associated with being old

D.V. – short for *deo volente*, Latin for 'God willing'

eminence – being of high rank, outstanding or distinguished

emoluments – salary, pay for work done

extenuation – an excuse, trying to make something look less serious

fain – willing, being glad to do something

foolscap – a sheet of paper, size 13 ½ x 17 inches (34 x 43 centimetres). The name came from the fool's (jester's) cap with bells, which was used as a watermark

inditing – writing, putting into words

in esse – Latin, in actual existence

initiatory – beginning, starting, introducing

in posse – Latin, a thing that could be possible

intractable – stubborn, difficult to deal with or manage

King's Bench prison – this was in Southwark in South London. The name came from the King's Bench law court, which tried offences such as slander, libel and bankruptcy, and the prison was often used for debtors. Imprisoning people for debt was stopped in the 1860s

lineaments – distinctive features or shapes, especially those of faces

lorn – forlorn, lost and sad

magnate – a powerful and important man

obdurate – stubborn, unyielding, hardened against persuasion

panorama – the word (from two Greek ones, meaning 'all view') was invented by the Irish painter Robert Barker, who had painted views of Edinburgh that were arranged in the shape of a cylinder, and viewed from inside. The viewer had to turn through 360° to see the complete scene. In 1793 Barker moved his paintings to a special panorama building in Leicester Square in London. Later Barker painted a panorama of London, which measured 250 square metres from end to end. Panoramas became very popular in nineteenth-century Europe and the United States

paragon – a model of perfection

paramount – supreme, of chief importance or concern

pecuniary – money, things to do with money and payments of money

Peregrine Pickle – a novel written in 1751 by the author Tobias Smollett. Peregrine Pickle is a wild young man who travels about and has all sorts of adventures – he is imprisoned in the Bastille, pretends to be a magician, tries to stand for Parliament, turns a beggar girl into a fine lady, and is imprisoned for debt in the Fleet prison. Finally he settles down, marrying a girl he has known for many years.

perusing – reading carefully, examining

playing Booty – a trick used by dishonest jockeys in which they look as though they are trying to win a race, but actually want to lose

portmanteau – a large leather suitcase that opens into two equal halves

posthumous – happening after death, such as a child born after his or her father dies, or a book published after the author's death

pound – a dialect version of 'expound', to explain

precept – a rule or command requiring a certain standard of behaviour

presentiment – a feeling that something is about to happen, a premonition

procrastination – putting off doing something until later

proctor – in a legal sense, a person conducting a case for someone else in the courts of canon or civil law. In a common law court, a proctor would be called a solicitor

profane – non-religious, worldly. Today it can mean vulgar, coarse, or treating something religious irreverently

profligacy – extremely extravagant or wasteful

prog – a slang word for food

quizzing glass – an eyeglass or monocle

repine – complain, be discontented

reticule – an old-fashioned handbag, a pouch usually made of net fabric and closed with a drawstring

stenography – the skill of writing in shorthand

stipend – a fixed amount of money paid at intervals for work done. It is also a clergyman's salary

surtout – a man's frock coat, with a single row of buttons and diagonal pockets

taciturn – not saying very much, uncommunicative

Tartar – a savage, fierce, bad-tempered person

ticket-porter – a member of a group of porters in the City of London who were licensed by the Corporation, the City's governing body

toll-man's apron – an apron worn by the men who collected tolls: the charges made for using certain roads and bridges. An apron with pockets was useful for storing money and keeping change

viands – food

woolsack – the seat used by the Lord Chancellor in Parliament. It is a huge leather cushion stuffed with wool, a symbol of the trade in wool and woollen cloth from which, for many centuries, England made its money